PHILLIPA PIPP
McINNES
Greensmith

CIRRUS WORTHY
Machinist

SIOBHAN SHIVERS
CLEARY
Navigator

CAM FALCONER
Windmaster

TARO CAT TAKESHI
Bladesmith

BROCK JONES
Wireman (ELECTRICIAN)

GWYNNE WICKLIFF
Aerologist

JESPER JAILBIR
GÖRANSSON
Junior Aerologi.

Flight of the Griffons

KATE INGLIS

ILLUSTRATIONS SYDNEY SMITH

NIMBUS
PUBLISHING LTD

Nimbus Publishing Limited
3731 Mackintosh St, Halifax, NS B3K 5A5
(902) 455-4286 nimbus.ca

Printed and bound in Canada
NB1120
Design: Heather Bryan

Library and Archives Canada Cataloguing in Publication

Inglis, Kate, 1973-, author
Flight of the griffons / Kate Inglis ; illustrations, Sydney Smith.

Issued in print and electronic formats.
ISBN 978-1-77108-132-0 (bound).—ISBN 978-1-77108-133-7 (pdf).—ISBN
978-1-77108-134-4 (mobi).—ISBN 978-1-77108-135-1 (html)

I. Smith, Sydney, 1980-, illustrator II. Title.

PS8617.N52F55 2014   jC813'.6   C2013-908108-9
                                   C2013-908109-7

Nimbus Publishing acknowledges the financial support for its publishing activities
from the Government of Canada through the Canada Book Fund (CBF) and
the Canada Council for the Arts, and from the Province of Nova Scotia through
Film & Creative Industries Nova Scotia. We are pleased to work in partnership
with Film & Creative Industries Nova Scotia to develop and promote our creative
industries for the benefit of all Nova Scotians.

For my sons, my parents, and all the makers, doers, and adventurers I've been so blessed to know.

Mother nature walks the woods trailing wet leaves and salt, her call as much the wing of a moth as a northeasterly howl. This story is for everyone who hears her, and is dedicated to every movement made—small, bold, perhaps a little mad—in her interest.

"*What* to do? It's hard to say, but when things are hard to say, you may as well start at the bottom and work your way up."

—Grampa Joe

Contents

Prologue

The pirate captain pressed the palm of his hand against metal, dragging it along until his fingertips found the fresh edge. It was still hot. He leaned in to peer through and out the other end, seeing stars, and shook his head at the thought of its intended volume. The ruptured pipeline was tall enough to walk through with only the slightest bend at the waist and promised profit as far as the eye could see to both horizons—until unfamiliar boots had hit the ground with a dusty thunk. *No bellyful of black gold for you,* he muttered. *Poison does not belong among pine and fox and whitetail doe.*

The pirate removed his hand and beckoned, gesturing to the rough cuts on either end of the twenty-foot section.

"Taro. Your file."

His bladesmith stepped forward, a power tool in hand, and bowed neatly.

"Smooth as silk, Captain. Four minutes."

The rotors of the outlawed ship spun slowly, a ready stance. The captain nodded and shouted over his shoulder.

"Four minutes."

Another voice replied, a domino effect.

"Crew to ship!"

Feet padded a light and urgent flurry around him, his crew making for stations and preparing for takeoff. He backed away slowly through the grass, appreciative of the craftsman who cauterized so diligently in the murk of early dawn. The metal shone and he studied it curiously. The act of cutting was forced domestication, an antidote to venom. *Now it's not a pipeline. It's just a pipe.* In a rain of sparks its progress had been amputated again, chopped as quickly as it grew thanks to his crew's steady-handed torches.

"*Bra jobbat!*" He raised a fist as he passed a brute standing high atop the pipe, who signalled back before throwing a carabiner full of cradle chains to another, who hauled it inside the fuselage to the anchoring bolt. His crew knew *well done* when they heard it. He strode purposefully up the ramp through narrow hallways lined with pliers, cutters, sticks of dynamite, bags of nails, strips of bolting steel, and mapped targets—the outfit of criminals or warriors, depending where you stood—until he reached his seat.

"Captain!" the pilot yelled over the accelerating chop of the rotors. "Shivers says Texada Island. As west as it gets until Japan. They'll never track it. Prevailing winds at the stern, but weather's coming up over the mountains."

The captain nodded, his eyes alight, and cupped his hands over his mouth.

"Jailbird!"

A slight, tall boy poked his head around the corner of the hatch, the wind whipping his hair.

"Did you see Grundy? Is Grundy aboard?"

"Yes, Captain." The boy pushed breathlessly across the cockpit threshold, his arms full of charts. "Hatches closed, all clear."

"*Res upp!*"

The Avenger lifted slowly, moving to hover over its cargo until the chains of the pipe's cradle snapped tight. Flight engineer, machinist, windsmith—one-by-one, all within the ship reached for anchors and portholes. It was a delicate business, sabotage of this scale.

"*Kom igen nu! DRA!*" The captain bellowed, and the ship heaved as the pipe swayed, airborne. The pilot pulled back on the throttle. In the cyclone of their departure a canvas note twirled violently until it settled in the grass.

A stinking rotten doom for your stinking rotten business. ~ G

He strained at the windshield to keep the destruction in sight as the Avenger banked, towing its prize through the night sky. He rose and pressed a thankful hand to the shoulder of his pilot and backed away, emerging into a mess of proud, steely faces.

"*God morgon*, pirates! One good day for us buys months of good days for the land. Now we drop this chopped snake and go to friends, *att söka skydd.* To the camp at 29!"

They cheered. The pilot's voice sounded, amplified from the cockpit.

3000 FEET AND HOLDING STEADY. CLOUD
COVER AFFIRMATIVE. BANKING FIVE DEGREES
PORT TO WEATHER. STEADY ON COURSE.

His coxswain clapped once, a cloud of metal dust jumping
from his hands.

"The sky!"

It was guttural, a battle cry—never in history had there been
a staging ground more desperate for warriors. *We fight for her.*
For mother earth we spite the industrial machine.

"The sky!" A chorus of voices replied. The ship shrank into
the horizon, the sky unruffled itself, and the disturbance was
gone.

• • •

"Mommy! Mommy!" The girl, all skinned knees and pigtails,
tumbled around the wooded corner. "You won't believe it there's
a helicopter! A great big one! Come see!"

Her mother, treasurer of the Texada Greenbelt Committee,
looked up in front of her basketful of yanked dandelions.
"What's that, sweetness? Yes, of course. That's nice."

"It's not nice, Mommy! It's a pirate ship!"

The red-faced girl talked with her hands, her arms splayed
wide in a gesture of some big thing. Her mother smiled and
bent again to her work.

"Muriel, love, you're in charge. You tell them they'd better be
friendly pirates if they're going to land on our island."

Her daughter, panting, blinked.

"Okay!" She scampered once more down the path. In the while that followed, Diane Falkenham pulled fistfuls of hawkweed, skeletonweed, leafy spurge. She sat up on her knees to wipe her brow, leaving a smear of dirt. It was almost suppertime.

"Muriel…" she called. "Mur—"

The whine of a turbine engine was followed by an unusual *thwap-thwap-thwap.*

"MURIEL!" She leapt to her feet, upturning the basket. She ran down the path and across the baseball diamond, then through the trees to the playground until she reared up on Charlie Moon, a fifth grader standing stock-still, his neck craned to the sky. She followed his gaze to the sound, still reverberating, an egg beater in churned-up clouds.

"That was cool," said Charlie, his hands in his pockets.

"Mommy!" (Mommy! Mommy!)

Her daughter appeared at the mouth of a long, silver tunnel that lay gleaming in the grass near the sandbox. Muriel ran through it back and forth, her sandals a flip-flapping echo, and she shrieked, giggling. Her mother approached, running trembling fingers across a brand cut into steel. *It can't be.*

A skull and crossbones.

Her shears clattered to the ground.

Chapter One

TERMS OF WORK

It was a day so brilliant with spring that even the abandoned grain elevators seemed cheerful. The union shuttle passed through the first set of gates and Missy grinned, remembering the last time she was here. It had been a couple of years ago, at dawn, on her way to stage the Dread Crew breakout with Eric (who was, as it happened, a surprisingly good picker of locks). Under his deft hand, the Barrow had rolled through a dozen seemingly impassable blockades. *It's a front*, he'd whispered at the first metal gate, flicking a mop of hair out of his face. In the shadow of the mammoth ship's wheel, he'd gestured at the obstacle in what turned out to be a classically Eric-like way, undeterred, eyes bright, using his screwdriver to punctuate. *It looks like you need a code, but you don't. You just take the facing off and pop the bolt.*

As they progressed through the industrial peninsula to its water-locked end, warehouses and trailers grew increasingly decrepit. Stray cats scattered and traffic diminished to lumbering characters who seemed roughworn in a way that went beyond the usual stevedores or crane operators who went home to board games and casseroles and heavy quilts.

As the shuttle stopped to turn, a small, white-haired man with skin like leather drove a forklift in the opposite direction. *Pirate*, thought Missy, her hand pressed against the glass. His eyes met hers for an instant, and in them she saw the same recognition. His face was expressionless, consumed in his task, but he gave a salute in her direction, two fingers to temple. Missy nodded back and then the forklift was gone, a flash of yellow disappearing in between two columns of sheet metal stacked ten feet high. The shuttle lurched forward and once again, Missy was filled with a rush of curiosity: *What happens next?*

• • •

"…That's nuthin' to the hurricanes. Last one flattened the whole park."

Again, the girl was unresponsive, her face pressed against the window. Ivan sighed, a little put out. He was a chatty sort, and nothing pleased him more than a like-minded passenger. *Never mind*, he thought to himself. *Kid's probably nervous, first time in front of the chief and all that.*

"Almost there, miss. You'll need your papers handy." In the rearview mirror the driver looked again at the girl, who was still fixed upon the view. "Miss?"

Waiting now to pass through the last gate, he turned in his seat, exasperated.

"Miss! Your papers." He snapped his fingers and the girl reacted, jarred by his movement. She dug in the small duffel she carried.

"Here." She offered a small booklet with an outstretched arm, and he took it.

• • •

The door featured a stencilled symbol meaningful only to those already initiated. It wasn't just the largest depot on the eastern seaboard. It was headquarters—source of orders, records, quotas, disciplinary actions. It was a holding cell for infractionists, a payroll office for everyone else. Pirate crews on this side of North America were bound to its infrastructure, for it housed the one thing that kept them protected and prosperous: their union. T.H.U.G.S.S., the Treasure Hunters & Useful  Goods Salvagers Society, was one part self-government, one part dictatorship, one part congregation of like minds, and wholly the most successful secret corporation in modern history. Chief B, boss of all captains, owned every ship and soul in her employ. She owned Hector Gristle, owned every Dread among his crew, and owned Missy Bullseye just the same.

Missy pushed the call button and placed her palm over the speaker's grill. It crackled against her skin and she paused for a suitable moment before responding.

"Missy Bullseye, reporting: probie local 52, uncertified 52-06-76. I have an eleven o'clock—"

The handle clicked in her fist as the door buzzed and popped open. She stepped through into a bureaucracy camouflaged on the outside by peeling paint and rust, its inside floors shining with institutional brilliance. Every last thing in sight was properly brisk, beige, and labelled. She was on the administrative level, after all, not on the depot floor among the pre-dismantled grit of the take.

A sign said RECEPTION →. She passed glass doors that led to pods of desks, catching glimpses here and there of the unfortunates obligated to an office workterm due to bad behaviour, bad records, or bad luck. She suppressed a giggle at the memory of Vince, the Dread Crew's first mate, in creased slacks and a hairnet. After she and Eric had broken the crew out of this very building, he'd saluted to her with a flourish every day for six months. *Well done, girl*, and he'd add *Bran cereal in the mornins, my livin' holy jeez, slap-five!* or *No more changin' the printer ink, slap-five!*, or *Roses on the cheeks, eh! Slap-five!* Union headquarters was any pirate's most necessary and most dreaded place—especially for those on the wrong side of the rules. Missy was not among that bunch, though, and so she felt as calm as she could given that she'd been the ringleader of the renowned breakout (still unsolved, officially, though the Dreads had been pardoned).

Probation. I just need probation so I can start, officially, so I can keep going. At the end of the hall, a neat man behind a desk looked up wearily. She took a breath.

"I—" Missy began, but he waved her to take a seat.

"They'll call you."

By the union's reckoning, waiting rooms and pirates had to reconcile, as well as all kinds of other things that don't go together—fax machines and pirates, filing cabinets and pirates, paperclips and pirates. This cramped box of carpeted cubicles seemed to squirm at its occupants, and its occupants squirmed back. A pair of brutes from some far-off place muttered behind their hands to one another. A bearded, long-haired man in coveralls drummed a small wrench in his hand as he reviewed a file, his posture indicating disagreement. A brass plaque mounted to a large brown door said CHIEF.

A young woman with a smear of black across the side of her face sat calmly, passing time as Missy did, and caught her eye.

"Workterm?" she gestured to the papers in Missy's lap.

"Yeah," Missy replied.

"Where did you go?"

"London. The Underground."

The pirate nodded approvingly. "First one?"

Missy nodded. "You?"

"Level three status, so far. Drilling engineer."

"With the Excavadoras?" Missy was fascinated.

"Nope," she snorted. "That's not drilling. That's burrowing. Bunch o' jungle moles, they are. No science to that bunch, they're just nuts. Good for laughs. My second term was with the Pokkas. Australia."

Missy's eyes widened. "Haven't heard of 'em."

"They hide in the outback, mostly. Pounce on cities, then retreat. They ride bangerangs. Half-diggers, half-trains. Bunch o' chutes an' tunnels get 'em away, back to the dirt. Odd bunch. Clever, though."

"What do they—"

The door that said CHIEF sprung open. A large man appeared and scanned the room.

"Bullseye." He pointed at her and flicked his wrist as though he were fishing. Missy leapt to her feet, knocking the chair with the backs of her knees.

Tilly "Twister" Gunn watched the slip of a thing make her way across neat industrial tile.

"Good luck," she called out. The girl didn't turn around.

• • •

A series of security camera screens filled a wall from floor to ceiling. Through the grey static of surveillance, pirates shuffled through the hangar, the receiving dock, the offices. Missy scanned the monitors for familiar faces. Then she felt rather than heard a presence and stiffened as a body brushed neatly past her chair. The woman who was chief turned to appraise the scarce-looking girl from across the polished desk. Missy appraised her in turn. The woman's shiny shoes, starched collar, and tight bun were those of a bureaucrat, not a pirate.

"You have already received your workterm assignment, have you not?" the chief nodded, answering her own question.

"Explain why you did not proceed as ordered."

"I made my way up to meet the Submariners, ma'am, like the letter said, after London, but they grazed a container off Helsinki and ripped the hull," Missy replied. "When I got there, they were already in drydock at the depot in Bremerhaven. So I couldn't fill my term with them."

The chief, expressionless, opened a file that had been placed in front of her. She ran one finger down one page and then another, her glasses perched on the end of her nose. After a pause, she spoke.

"Noted. You will not fulfill your apprenticeship, and only two work terms will not accumulate the required study credits. You will not reach probationary status this season."

Missy pushed away a sudden, despairing urge to run. She thought of jungle moles. "What about the Excavadoras?"

"They are in an unstable region of the Ecuadorean south, and cannot surface."

"The Bom…"

She cut Missy short. "The Bombadiers are in refit. They've been given a Conditional Leave of Absence until the snowpack firms up. They will not be free of it anytime soon, knowing the Cariboo region."

The chief turned her attention again to the file in front of her.

"Alaisdair Black found you useful," she said, more to herself than the deflated girl in front of her. "Two months on the rails…junior welder on *Kingsgut IV*, running chains on *Lord*

Dowdy, greaser on *Biggin Hill*. They treated you well?"

Missy nodded.

"And how did you enjoy a locomotive life?" She winked, and Missy stiffened.

"Fine, ma'am." It was only the slightest of lies. She preferred open air to damp and darkness, but Missy was a stubborn sort, and didn't like being winked at. "Londoners have got no idea how big London really is."

"Indeed. Takes all the reasoning we've got to prevent those braggarts from inviting citizens down for a look, so proud they are of their tunnel city." She shook her head and flipped through Missy's submitted papers, muttering to herself.

"You were to report to the Crummies for your third and final term, correct?"

"Yes, ma'am."

"Do that now, then. The Crummies will serve as your second term. I'll have them located, and one of our transports will bring you to Fort MacKenzie. This will complete two-thirds of your apprenticeship. We will find you another placement next year. That is all."

Missy sank in her chair. *Another year of not bein' a certified scrapper. Still just a stowaway.* It had grated on her all these years, not being recognized. She had dropped her muddy, scrawny self onto the top deck of the Barrow and argued her right to stay, if only for her lack of anywhere else to go. Then she got a taste for wreckage. Then she saw fit to earn her keep, which required more of her eyes and wits than it did of every other soul on that ship put together. And so she watched the maps, the mechanics, the woods. She became an interventionist, preventing more than one unwanted crash. She found lost bolts and new targets, got to know junk and its value. She snuck into captain's quarters after every briefing to review the union memos herself. She kept a keen eye on Gristle as he consulted with Meena, his navigator, or Vince, his first mate. She watched his every intent, frustration, change in tone. He would give the order and the ship would turn. She was still a muddy, scrawny thing, but Missy Bullseye— the name they'd given to her—had became indispensably proficient. As she became more versed in the study of splinters and junk, she became more hungry. It had grabbed onto her at the base of her spine, the hustle that followed captain's orders.

The chief turned in dismissal, reaching to the cabinet behind her desk for a stack of rebar remittance or disciplinary filing or whatever administrative task awaited her next.

"Ma'am…" The chief looked up, pestered. Missy settled on the very last name she could muster. "The G-G-Griffons."

The chief's eyes narrowed. "What about the Griffons?"

"They cross over into Crummy territory, don't they? Could I… couldn't I finish up with them?"

There was a long silence as the boss of all captains scrutinized the impatient girl who stood before her. *Is she mocking? Or does she not know?* The earnest hope on the girl's face indicated the latter.

"The Griffons are blacklisted." She spoke in a measured tone. "They are defectors. Criminals. Even if you could find them—which you could not—they would be unsuitable for an apprenticeship in every possible way."

She watched as something was lit inside the girl, and recognized something of herself—a rebellious nature ignited by the words *you cannot*. She paused, and in that pause the girl made one final appeal.

"I've got nothin' to lose. Neither do you. The Dreads are pullin' in more junk now than they ever did. They're fine without me for a bit longer after I'm done with the Crummies. You might as well let me at the blacklist. Last known location, ship specs. Whatever you've got."

Chief rose from her desk and came out from behind it to stand in front of the girl, tapping the end of a pen on her palm.

"You understand this is absurd," she said. Missy nodded. "You understand we have been hunting this crew for nearly a decade now with hardly a whiff of them."

Missy nodded again.

"You understand they are airborne."

"I know that, ma'am. But they've been runnin' from you— from a big union mess—for ages. They're not expectin' one kid. If I find 'em I'll stay with 'em so I know what they're up to and where they go. I'll report back and in return, I want that workterm credit. I want probationary status."

The woman crossed the room to the wall of cabinets, tracing

her finger across the codes that labelled each one. She pulled
open one of the drawers and from it retrieved a series of black
folders, each marked RESTRICTED, and dropped them onto
the desk in front of Missy.

"You will complete your second workterm. Then, you
have two weeks to provide us with a verifiable lead as to
the whereabouts of Rasmus Krook and his crew. If you are
successful, I will waive the third workterm requirement. Do you
understand?"

"Yes, ma'am."

The chief looked squarely at the girl, jabbing one finger into
the air. "Mine will be your first and only mandate, should you
get even the faintest sign. You are owned by me and me alone."

Missy's stomach turned. "Yes, ma'am."

As they delved into stacks of memos, maps, and reports all
stamped red with CONDEMNED IN ABSENTIA, Missy's
whole being shrank with shame. A pile grew for her perusal,
undercover intelligence to help recover a renegade crew. And she
would help them do it. No longer was she a friend of pirates.

Missy Bullseye was a turncoat.

• • •

The incident file, laid out on the chief's desk, was as much a
taunt now as ever. She slipped the edge of a fingernail through
the black tape that sealed it shut and flipped the cover, past
a page that said RESTRICTED ACCESS, a stamp that
said OUTSTANDING WARRANT, and a chronological

chart peppered with X's that concluded, at the bottom left: CONTINUED FAILURE TO REPORT. She flipped through an inch-thick stack of police bribes, internal reports, marked-up maps, clippings, and investigative analyses, finally settling to tug on an edge with a telltale glossy finish. The personnel file.

RASMUS KROOK, CAPTAIN, LEVEL-1 CERTIFIED. LICENSE FOR PIRACY #61-01-01 [REVOKED NOVEMBER 2002]. *It can't have been ten years, damn him, but it is.* He'd been ruddy, but somehow refined. Dimples, set charmingly. A smallish kind of man, at least in a row of pirate captains. But he still seemed tall, somehow. She imagined he'd be much the same these years later, with perhaps more wind and weather in the lines of his face. She shook off the imagining contemptuously.

"Scum," she snarled at the photo. Even expressionless, as all subjects were instructed to be for officer identification, he smirked.

"I should have known," Chief spoke out loud to the empty room. Perhaps she'd missed some elemental difference, a dysfunctional glint in his eye or manner or conduct. But *what* should she have known, had she noted a red flag? That he was a liability? That after all the years it took to turn a gang profitable, he'd disappear with no regard for her investment? That he'd abscond with one of the most evasive ships in the history of the union, taking one of its most prolific crews with him? And to what end? He was unhuntable, uncatchable, a stick in her craw as much as a tantalizing figurehead for dissatisfied scrappers. She'd heard their whispers over the years. She made a point of it.

"I'll find a stick to put in *your* craw, Krook, wherever you are," she muttered, half-declaring it and half-wishing it, divided as to which it was.

Chapter Two

FAREWELL, WHERE ALL BEGINNINGS ROOT

"*Make* it big." Johnnie spoke to Ike with a softness rather than a bite. "Chop up that dead spruce behind the barn to start. Joe's wanted it gone anyways. Then dig into that stack of applewood, good and hard. Thrown onto a fire started hot, it'll burn long. Let's send her off right."

Ike sniffed and nodded, but didn't move.

"Look, Ike, I feel the same way. She gets back from London when the snow melts and then boom, it's May and she's off again. But it's what she's got to do. You had to, and so did I. Workterms make it official." Johnnie gave a gentle nudge to the brute's shoulder. "Here. I'll get the saw and give you a hand."

It was a solemn day for Dread Crew pirates. There were no barked orders, no insults, no carelessness that caused machines and mouths to backfire. Bodies shuffled quietly and without complaint, all focused on the preparation of saying goodbye once more to their daughter, the girl with such promise. Johnnie braced the dead tree while Ike laid the blade across the trunk. The tongueless brute widened his stance and began to saw, a stream of dust shooting out as the teeth bit into wood. *She's the only one that helps me talk.*

Johnnie lowered his eyes. He knew what Ike was thinking, and that got him to thinking too. *She's so small.*

Across the yard, Ewsula rolled a petrified log toward the firepit for a bench. *She don't need us no more. She was wily in London. She'll be wily anywhere.*

Sam buckled under the weight of two cast-iron pots called to fireside for the brewing of malted milk. *Must 'member to check her pack. Girl throws everything in there like dog's breakfast. Plus I got those socks I knit for 'er. Girl's gonna need warm feet.*

• • •

It was a cloudy day, but every now and then a brilliant beam of sun would crack through, shining a spotlight. For a moment the kitchen window was illuminated and Anneke Stewart, mother of a pirate-tracker-turned-conspirator, stopped kneading.

"I hope these clouds break up," she peered up at the sky through panes of glass. "Last thing we want is rain on Missy's last night."

Zeke glanced through the window as he passed, a sack of flour in his arms. "Hmmm," he mumbled. "Where's that cornmeal? You said it's good grit for hardtack, and she's gonna need extra for the trip..."

They'd been in the house kitchen all afternoon working side by side, Eric's mother and the Dread Crew's slopjack. Two cooks, one of leech jelly and stinging cracklebread and the other of everyday buckles and roasts, she to whom the kitchen belonged. But there they were, pounding and rolling and stirring together, comparing philosophies, chatting all the while.

Zeke raised his eyebrows at her before reaching into a bottle of solomon gundy with bare hands. She smiled and gestured permission. He'd eaten almost all of it already as it was. His hand came up dripping with brine, a slop of pickled herring between his fingers. He dropped it into his mouth and wiped his hands on his apron, sighing contentedly.

"I'm not one for fish unless it's eel, anyone'll tell you that. But this is good stuff. Puts hair on yer chin."

Anneke passed him a mason jar of cornmeal as well as another bundle, and he took both.

"You might want to add some of those dried blueberries, too," she said. "I think she'll get a kick out of that. Blue hardtack."

Zeke nodded, though he preferred salty over sweet. *Whatever she likes she gets today, our girl.*

• • •

Missy hadn't grown up with Slip 'n Slides and Popsicles and a homeroom bell. Eric had figured that out from the moment she'd climbed through his window that night two years back. He could tell it from her boots. She was feral. *You're a tracker,* she'd said, giving him something between a sneer and a grin. *I'm a pirate.* The Dread Crew found old Joe to be useful and the neighbouring Stewart homestead, sprawling with old woodlot and plenty of feral-friendly places, to be just right. They plundered as usual (though, thanks to Joe, with somewhat more savvy), and collected junk for union remittance. Life had become almost ordinary—even with the giant wheelbarrow ship, the smashed leech jam at breakfast, and the thirteen-year-old girl who'd never ridden a bike before.

He had spent the morning running along behind her, sheep-dogging her away from ditches and potholes as she wobbled on one of his old ones. She'd gotten the hang of it. Now, on the eve of her farewell party, they rode together into New Germany for sea salt, an urgent mission or a manufactured errand depending on your point of view. Every now and then he'd turn to check on her, his own bike swaying, being her ears and watching for traffic, signalling *Keep going. This way. Take a left. Watch out.* The pavement turned to gravel and narrowed, a road demoted to a lane. They passed through an iron gate that was ajar and Missy saw a sign.

NORTH FORK GARRISON. CIRCA 1832.

Ducking under the reach of trees and into a clearing rimmed with stonework, Eric stopped at the bottom of a grassy mound. He swung one leg over and steadied the bike, digging in the panniers. With a paper bag in one hand and two cans of ginger ale in the front pocket of his hoodie, he let his bike down to the ground. He gestured for her to follow, and they set off up the hill until Missy found herself looking down the barrel of a gun.

"A cannon!" she exclaimed, instinctively moving aside from its mouth.

"Yeah," said Eric. "There's piles of 'em. This is where the British used to store the signal guns. Not any of the heavy artillery."

Beyond the mound was another hollow, an outdoor bunker so large that it contained several small sheds, watchposts, and soldiers' quarters. Eric hopped up onto one of the larger stone walls, pulled both cans out of his pocket, and set them on the grass. Crows circled and landed, then circled again. Missy felt it strange that a place built for war could be so peaceful, or perhaps at how thoroughly a place built for war could be overtaken by dandelions. She liked it very much. He sat down, and so did she.

Eric spoke as neatly as he could, his mouth full of oatcake. "Are you nervous?"

Missy shrugged. She was chewing. He waited.

"A little," she said after a while. "But they were all me, once. Beginners. No point worryin' about it."

"Do you ever wonder if…" Eric halted. "Never mind."

Missy never minded. He tried again.

"I never asked because I didn't know how to, not without making you think that I think that…you can't…but when you were away on the trains, was hearing ever a problem? Or, not being able to hear? Like, something that would keep you from being safe—"

"I'm never safe. Neither are you. Nobody is." She had a way of blurting out true things that churned in Eric's head for days. "I'm mostly deaf. Some people are all deaf. Lots of people wander around without all their parts workin'. Brains and eyes and ears and feet. Lots of people look like they're workin' but they're not."

She tipped the can up at her mouth and drank, swallowed, and continued. "It's not like anybody chooses what they are. You get what you get. But you just got to keep goin', 'cause why not?"

They sat there a long time. They talked about the biggest blizzards they could remember, and about secret tunnels under London, and about how Eric wanted to race mountain bikes like Chris Rushton, the high school kid who lived in New Germany. They talked about the most disgusting thing they'd ever eaten (Missy thought herself unbeatable on that front, but she was not). They ran from storeroom to turret in search of old barrels and iron scraps. They hunted for ghosts until the sun sank behind the trees and that sinking brought with it a chill that called them home.

Growing more confident, Missy pedalled ahead through a clearing of weeds until her tires reached the crushed rock of the road and she stopped there, turning to confirm that he followed. After stuffing the empty cans and paper bag back into his panniers, Eric grasped the handlebars and kicked off from the ground.

How did it get to be six o'clock?

•••

"Well?" Anneke wiped her brow with a forearm. Her hair was pinned back, her apron smeared with a full day of good work. Zeke's was too. The cooks stood together, looking expectantly at delinquent suppliers. "The salt, Eric! That's the whole reason you two went out. All we have is fine grind. Zeke says biscuits are better with coarse and I'm inclined to agree."

Eric turned to look at Missy, who hadn't been paying attention. Her face had gone soft, watching through the kitchen window at people streaming through the driveway gates with blankets and chairs.

"We forgot." Eric's face had gone soft, too. His mother shook her head.

"Gah! Fine it is, then. Sorry, Zeke. I have a son with a head full of rocks."

Frankie, called to the kitchen with an order of cream from the cold cellar, smiled. *That's not rocks.*

• • •

Filled up with food and drink, pirates and neighbours gravitated to a noisy and cheerful array at the bonfire. It swirled up, ribbons of orange and red licking the sky, cracking and popping in the consumption of wood. It was the heart of the night. Through the flames Eric saw his dad, Dan, tuning his guitar. Vince appeared from behind the stern of the ship. He was carrying a very old banjo. Eric and Missy sat together on an old horse blanket. He nudged her.

"Vince plays?"

"Sure does," she replied. Bodies grew thick around them, shoulder to shoulder, backs propped against friendly knees. People stood in clusters, chatting and milling about. Children huddled around the lighter of an obliging grown-up, holding sparklers steady until they burst into a spitting brightness, one then the next and then two more and three. They hooted and ran, weaving through the crowd trailing white-hot sizzle streaks in the night.

Dan began to strum. Then another guitar joined, and a ukulele, a banjo—stringed cousins weaving together around the thump of Joe's box bass. Vince, the most dour of the Dreads most days, led the song.

> *Every day before breakfast her mother said daughter*
> *It's time you got yer bucket and went to fetch water*
> *And she'd skip down the path to the cool, dark eddy*
> *that fed into the Caney Fork River*

As he sang, the only hint of his usual demeanour was his shut-tight eyes. The rest of him was all pride from his posture to his pluck, brought on by the fire.

> *Well the log struck a rock and I went to the bottom*
> *And my body washed away late last autumn*
> *My spirit still lingers in the cool dark water*
> *That washes the skin of Ferguson's daughter*

Eric's eyes dropped to Missy's boots. Her legs were crossed at the ankles, littered with scratches and bruises. He retraced his memory, seeing in flashes the happening of a few of them, a badly hammered nail head or a rope burn or a heavy thing that had snapped shut on a piece of her. She'd sprained her wrist shortly after coming on board at nine years old. She'd told him the story of it once. It hadn't healed properly and the bone there jutted out, but only if you knew to notice.

Almost four years had passed since she'd found her way on board. With the exception of her time in London, she'd never been away from the ship or its pilots. *They're not like mothers and fathers*, she'd explained a while back. *They don't fuss over me or over anybody. They're more like… uncles and aunts. Except I wasn't born to 'em. I picked 'em. Yeah. I got eleven uncles and three aunts and we all live together and it's real messy.*

Beside him, Missy's boots swayed in time with the song. He nudged her again and she turned to him.

"You can hear?"

"Course not, dope." She nudged him back. "They do this whenever they stop somewhere. They get off ship and they're all itchy fingers. For me it's like watching poems. I can see the beat. Reminds me of my dad."

Eric wondered about her dad. They hadn't ever talked about him.

"Anyway, hearing's not the right word," she continued. "The music changes the air."

Amos had sidled next to Vince, showing all his teeth. He raised his glass to Missy, and she smiled broadly in return. He took a deep breath, joining in for the chorus.

Caney Fork River, Caney Fork River
Water everywhere, it's a taker and a giver…

In the space between the last note and what should have

been applause, a lone goat watching through the fence called
MEEEEHH!

"Heckler!" Ewsula bellowed. The goat snorted. The rest
happened very quickly. Ewsula leapt to her feet. So did Ike. The
two of them charged the pen, the rest of the pirates on their
feet too. In one leap Sula hurdled the fence, scattering goats like
ducks in a pond. Everyone was in hysterics now. Ike hopped the
fence too and the goats were a pandemonium of spindle legs, fat
bellies, and beady-eyed outrage.

"Git over 'ere, devils!"

MEEEH! MEEH!!

Sula tackled the offender and came up with Gaetane—the
one Eric's dad called Holy Goat for all his yanging—tucked
under one arm like a football. Gaetane squirmed and kicked.
Eric looked sideways at Missy. She was holding her stomach,
laughing, tears streaming down her face. She jumped up from
the blanket and ran to the fence, leaping up to stand taller and
clap. Two more joined her, younger girls from Eric's school.
Missy cupped her hands over her mouth.

"Give us a show, Sula!"

The younger girls, gazing adoringly at Missy, leaned over the
fence.

"Yeah, S-Sula! Give us a show!" they cried.

"ROOOWREEEH!" The barbarian roared victory and
Gaetane went begrudgingly limp. Ike, panting, stood with
hands on his knees in the middle of three goats who, the chase

abandoned, chewed on the leg of his coveralls. He made a show of trying to escape and was promptly pinned to the ground by hooves and nuzzling noses. Ewsula ruffled the fur on the top of Gaetane's head and let go just as he nipped at her hand. The goat bounced and trotted off, a vision of rebuttal, and the brute bowed deeply.

"Hear, hear!" Vince waved his banjo above his head. "Let it be known to all hecklers what fate they seek among Dreads!"

The neighbourhood's huddle of kids, moms, dads, teachers, dairy farmers, and junk pirates cheered. Missy and her admirers hopped off the fence and ran together for the ship. *They love it when she lets them up the chain net,* Eric thought, and then he frowned a little. *She's going to miss this.*

• • •

The night grew blacker and blacker still, and the fire higher and more bright. Frankie drummed on an upturned barrel. Two of Eric's friends from soccer manned the popcorn maker, and the scent of butter swirled through the air. Preschoolers up past bedtime took turns sneaking up on Sam, who swatted them away, growling ferociously and pretending to doze off so they could bother him again. Zeke and Eric's mother passed out s'mores in tinfoil bundles for the fire's perimeter. Handing one to Eric, Zeke leaned in.

"Don' tell yer ma, but I added a bit. Can't have fudge wit'out a bit o' kick."

"Fine by me." Eric smiled. "Just don't tell me what's in it."

The cook slapped him approvingly on the back. "Adventurous lad, that boy is!" Zeke disappeared through the crowd with his basket.

Eric contemplated the packet of tinfoil in his palm. *It's either fire pepper or spider legs for crunch. What's that he calls it? Grit for your gizzard.* He laid one on the coals, and another for Missy.

Chapter Three

ON THE ROAD

Those among the crew who weren't dousing the fire, rounding up animals, or sniffing around for half-eaten plates gathered up in the attic, as was their habit. It had been laid with thick carpets, ratty leftovers from here and there, and Dan and Eric had built long, wide benches with a table in the middle for the laying-out of charts and food. Some of the bigger pirates had to crouch, and a meeting never reached its conclusion without at least one bumped head or knocked elbow. But with brass hurricane lanterns mounted on the walls and flea market quilts to soften the wood, what had been Eric's solitary hideout was now a clubhouse for thugs—and a cozy one, too.

Missy sat cross-legged in the middle of the table.

"Maybe I should stay. You need a crew that's ten times ten, right? All-in? Like you said. Gotta keep up this streak."

It had grown quiet in the attic. In the morning, Eric's father would bring Missy to headquarters and from there, she'd be delivered to parts unknown. Throughout the evening they'd drowned out the imminence of her departure with banjos and marshmallows, but it was now upon them. She would leave an empty hole.

"No, Miss Mairi." Hector drew deeply on one of Joe's pipes, dwarfed between his fingers, and exhaled a cloud of smoke that hung in the air around his face. "You came aboard…what was it? Four years back or more? All I wanted was for you to go on your way but you stuck like a belly on a goat. I'm startin' to think we suit you."

Missy narrowed her eyes. "You suit me as fine as you need me."

Her captain bit again on the end of the pipe. *Child's got a gumption that needs its own ship.*

"We oughta add up all the times that kid's kept us wheel-side down." Gretchen had a voice like sandpaper, but just now it was nearly soft. Missy had missed it, Gretch being against the wall and in shadow. But she didn't need to hear to see the agreement that rippled through the room. Missy shifted, fiddling with the hem of her shirt until Hector rapped on the table.

"Listen, girl. You're Dread. Until you get your own, the Barrow is your post, no matter what levels or papers or probations. You's one of us. Whatever happens in months comin' is schoolin', just like you did in the Underground. They took a care of you, those Blitzes, and you did us proud. And you'll do it again. You'll be on the sea or in the caves or hoppin' glaciers or trawlin' factories an' then back to us. In the meantime, get us news yerself. I don' trust those bureaucrats. And you be Dread, wherever you get to, same as always. This night was no goodbye. This night was a see-you-soon."

She fixed him into her mind's eye. The snakes of his beard that shook a little as he spoke. The way he smelled like sap and dregs of jerry cans. Eyes dark with years. The heft of him as he walked, feet pressing into earth, everything before him bowing or trembling, as everything should.

Before long, pirates made their way to berths and cots and tents—but only after finding Missy for a pat on her back, last-minute advice, and reminders they knew she didn't need but gave her anyway. *Work hard. Keep your eyes peeled.* She was the last down the attic steps and the steep kitchen stairs, minding those that creaked. Eric's parents had long since gone to bed, resting for dawn's drive into the city. Lights had been doused, dishes piled in heaps. As she opened the door into the breezeway, where the walls were stacked high with tubs of goat cheese, three kittens usually poised to dart through unwatched doors lay on a pillow in a lolling, furry tangle. One lifted its head as if to say *Open that again tomorrow, will you?*

Missy replied as she always did. *Fsss, fsss, fsss* and a click of her tongue. She slipped outside and made her way to the Barrow. At its base she could smell tar, grease, the tang of metal, the goodness of wood. She reached out to grasp the chain when she felt a tap on her shoulder. It was Joe, standing there with Eric.

"A good night, Missy? Never seen a finer send-off, myself."

"Never had that before. The pirates, you know, they don't stop for birthdays or holidays or nothin'. Only for hot dogs. Not that I mind. But that was great."

"No one's ever thrown you a party?" As she shook her head, Eric was reminded of just how unconventional Missy was. Her dad, not attuned to normal stuff, had taught Missy how to catch a fish with her bare hands. She'd had to pick up the rest on her own.

"I'm off to bed, Missy," Joe gestured for her attention. "Told Dan I'd go along tomorrow morning, bright an' early. We're going to stop off at the steel fabricator's on the way back. Sam took Sula over there last week for new gun braces and they went all vinegar. So we gotta go over there and be all honey. Night, scout."

Joe embraced her quickly, knowing she tended to skittishness like one of Bertha Pringle's cats. (He had pipe ash in his chest pocket, and her nose squashed up against it. She inhaled. *I bet this is what grampas smell like.*)

Joe pulled away and turned into the darkness toward his cabin, leaving Eric and Missy under the porch light. Eric thrust his hands in the pockets of his jeans. There was a small, smooth rock in the right one that was perfectly round. *Every wanderer needs a good rock in his pocket,* Joe had told him once. *Keeps your head from runnin' away.* He rubbed the edges of it with his thumb.

"You gonna send postcards again?"

"Yeah. Don't know how close I'll be to a mailbox, though."

Eric wondered what she'd look like without dirt on her face. *Wouldn't be her.* He cleared his throat. "Bye, Missy. Have a good trip."

"'Night, tracker." She looked at her boots, one toe held together with duct tape, and suddenly felt very much like a strange girl, but there was nothing to be done about that. She turned for the ship and he for the house. Climbing up and over the lip of the deck, she looked once more to see the screen door spring shut behind him and the porch light go to black.

• • •

By the time she'd reached the Ontario border, Missy knew exactly how long a kilometre was. Sixteen unforced blinks. Pirates and officials climbed in and out of the van on a milk run of union errands. They dropped off two in Edmunston. They met the ferry at Rivière-du-Loup bound for Saint-Siméon, then drove up to Chicoutimi for a pickup who never showed, then collected a packet of documents in Drummondville. Nights and days blurred together. Every now and then a bundle from Tim Horton's was handed back to her, or she'd get out for air and a stretch at a rest stop. Then she was gruffly ordered back into the van and slid across grey vinyl to her seat to buckle in and prop her feet on her backpack.

No one spoke much. She stared out the window at tired convenience stores and collarless dogs tramping through Trans-Canada towns. Then the pickup of a box of paperwork in Sudbury, a hushed conversation in Sault Ste. Marie, and from there, they turned further north to smaller towns, thicker forest, and ditches lined with foraging moose. She saw hunters in orange vests and wished the animals stealth. Signs said

482 KMS TO NEXT GAS and where highways intersected
she saw alternate routes stretching out into an unending
boreal forest, some paved and some not. On the turnoff from
Kapuskasing, the nameless driver popped open the back door
to store a few gallons of extra fuel at Missy's back. Then onto
the highway again—a smaller one to an offshoot, then from the
offshoot to an access road. The road had gone wild, and it was
here—underneath a sign that said ABITIBI CANYON 5—
where the van finally shuddered to a stop.

The driver climbed down from his seat and slid the panel
door open. "Out you get."

She hopped outside, heaving her pack onto her back, and
stared blankly at the van. "Here?"

The union driver smacked a mouthful of chewing gum.
"There's an old hydro station abandoned in 1980 down the end
of that road. Crummies made it theirs. Got a few houses an' a
hockey rink an' everythin'. Just shells left, but it's dry. Road hasn't
been touched since then and it's cracked too bad for anythin' but
four-wheel drive. Anyways, they'll be here soon. Headquarters
had a GPS signal on 'em leavin' Kesagami Lake up north."

Missy wondered about people this far north saying "up north."

"Our timin' is…" He checked his watch more for show than
anything else. "Jus' right."

He rounded the van to the driver's side and climbed back
up behind the wheel. She followed, lingering beneath the open
window.

"Stay put. If yeh don't see 'em soon, there's a satellite phone attached to the pole." He gestured at the sign for the canyon. "But don't use it unless yeh must. An' don't worry. There's no grizzlies 'round here. Jus' skinny blacks an' all they eat is berries, not pirates. But don't scare 'em. They'll take a chunk outta yeh if they're scared."

Through the window he thrust a crumpled grocery bag into her hands and pulled away without another word. The van turned in a circle around her before retreating back down the road. Through the rearview window she saw him give a stiff wave. She waved back, but by then he was already gone. Missy was alone, dropped unceremoniously at the beginning of a ghost town's road with a half-drunken bottle of orange juice, four stale Timbits, a banana, and a bag of salt-and-vinegar chips.

ABITIBI CANYON 5. The sign straightened its back, unaccustomed to being looked at. The girl took a few steps toward it, then dropped her pack at its base. Beyond the sign was a curtain of evergreens just thick enough to be unremarkable to passing cars, if there were any passing cars, which there weren't, but Missy knew better. Through the trees she saw a collection of trailers, a padlocked mishmash of corrugated steel and sheet siding. A handmade sign in one of the windows said KEEP OUT. Graffiti scrawl on another said TEDDY BEAR PICNIC. 5 KM AHEAD.

What kind of ship is it? she had asked. The driver shook his head, and she thought she'd seen him say "no ship." She paced for an hour, maybe two. She pulled a fleece over her head and took it off again. She walked in circles and ate chips. *A crew can't be a crew without a ship. "New ship"? Maybe that's what he said.* The trailers made her uneasy. Finally, she sat on the ground at the base of the sign and waited for something to happen.

Chapter Four

CRUMMY DAY

The truck rolled toward her from the wild end of the road, rocking and tipping uphill and downhill across ruts and washouts. She stood and walked to the dividing line. The truck slowed and stopped. She lifted her backpack to her shoulder and raised one hand into the air. The truck idled, staring Missy down, its driver obscured behind glass and filth, its exhaust forming a cloud like breath on a brisk morning. Massive tires encased in a net of chains were half-sunk in the late spring mud beyond where the asphalt stopped. She took a step forward and then another before reaching into her back pocket. She brought her hand up, clutching her union papers, and waved for permission to advance. The exhaust coughed and the engine stopped. She walked to the end of the pavement and forward through soft, wild dirt, straining under the weight of her pack but still holding the papers high. Then the door opened and a man jumped out, landing heavily.

He looked agitated. He was speaking to her, but she was too far away to read him. *I have to get closer. He doesn't know I have to be closer.*

"Are you with the…" She continued to walk forward, gesturing to the truck. "Are you a pir—"

The man answered but again, he was too far away. He gestured to his watch, to the road, to whatever load he carried inside the truck.

"Wait," she shouted again and picked up her pace, running toward him as lightly as she could. He shifted on his feet, his arms folded across his chest. Finally she stood in front of him, a man dressed thick in well-worn plaid, his hair caked with mud and sap and grease, the sweat of the forest. He stared at her with a stern look on his face. Panting, she handed him her papers, and he took them.

"I'm Missy," she said. "I'm the new apprentice."

He scanned the papers, expressionless. "International pirates? A…union? What the heck is this?"

Missy was stunned into silence. She hurriedly took him in. *A logger? A miner? What else is up here?*

"Is this some kind of joke?" He shook the papers into her face. She gulped. "Two factories robbed, a decommissioned mine looted, and three cell towers dismantled for steel, all in the past month. What do you know of pirates, girl? Explain yourself!"

He yelled at her. She needed no volume to know it. Missy instinctively moved backwards without taking her eyes off the man. Then her field of vision cleared and suddenly she knew what to do. She giggled.

"Ease up, buddy. It's only a joke. Some friends dared me to

do it. They were just over there but they ran away when they saw your truck."

"Oh, they did, did they?" He clutched the papers. "You and your friends, what're you doin' way out here on your own?"

"We live in…Kapuskasing. My big brother drove us up here. We're training for a big hike. We're doin' the P-Pictou Trail next summer."

"Pictou? I know all the trails round here. Never heard of it."

Don't stop looking at him. "Yeah. It's new. Long-distance hike. We're takin'…orient…orientation at school. In class. In Kapuskasing. We're studying it. Maps and stuff."

He glared at her. "Orienteering, you mean?"

"Yeah. Yeah, that's it."

"You're from Kapuskasing?"

"Yeah."

"You're in school?"

"Yeah."

"You're a pirate?"

"Yeah."

Missy clapped her hand over her mouth. The man pointed at her, triumphant.

"I knew it! You're a pirate." Missy backed up. She blinked. *Good lord. Oh good lord.* But then he grinned. "So am I."

He loosened his grip on her papers and reached a hand out in greeting.

"Eli Bottom. The Bishop. Jury-rigger with the Crummies."

She stared at his outstretched hand, her chest still pounding.

"I'm sent here to pick you up. They told us you were on yer way. That there's my scrap truck. You're catchin' flies, Missy-girl. Gotcha good, eh?"

Missy snapped her mouth shut and shook her head. She put her hand into his and gave it a feeble squeeze.

"Nobody's ever gotten me like that."

"Ah, yeh. I can't help meself. Here—lemme take yer pack."

"I'm okay." She wrapped her hand around the shoulder strap.

"'Atta girl. Truck's knee-deep in wrappers an' pop cans right now, sorry to say, but we'll…" He turned toward the truck mid-sentence. Scrambling to follow, she watched the back of his head bob up and down and side to side like his ambling truck. He was still talking.

"Eli," she called. He turned around as he opened the door. "You've got to face me when you talk to me. I don't hear too well."

He gave her a thumbs-up. "Got it. Let's go!"

With a deep breath she threw her pack into the back of the truck and hoisted herself into the cab, delivered.

•••

The road evened a little, though still unpaved, and the truck picked up speed. "So you're a Dread, are you?"

"I am," she replied.

"They're like us, I hear," he said. "Except they jus' got the one ship. What a ship, though. Everyone knows the Barrow. Mick says he met your captain and a few others at headquarters, eh?"

"Yeah, I think he did." Missy watched as Eli reached into the glovebox for a toque and pulled it onto his head.

"Cold front comin' in," he said. "The window's stuck open. You want one?"

"Sure," said Missy, shivering. He handed her a woven black hat with bright green letters across the front. HUSQVARNA.

"We raided a power equipment warehouse once. There was a basket of 'em by the front door. Everyone never shut it about me takin' hats instead o' chainsaws. But out here, if yer not warm, yer useless, an' even in June I seen frost at breakfast."

Missy pulled it over her head.

"So tell me." He turned toward her. "What'd the Dreads do to get the whole lot of 'em thrown into the clink?"

Missy recounted the story of Joe's hoard, and the revelation that pirates could be honey instead of vinegar, nice instead of rude, and get more scrap that way. And the festival—Joe's idea—the thousands of people dressed like pirates, thinking it fun, and bringing all their junk. The mountain of junk! And the white vans of the union, how they thought the Dreads had been coasting. And how they all ran but got caught, and how the Dreads got hauled away to headquarters, and how Missy and a tracker kid hijacked the Barrow and busted them out, and how the tracker kid's name was Eric, and how he was just a normal boy, not a pirate at all, but he steered the most notorious ship ever known all the way out the warehouse to freedom.

Eli listened intently, shaking his head all the while and interjecting with things like *You don't say!* and *Ordinary folk?* and *I never seen that before* and *Oh, that's off!* and *What then?*

"…And that's it." She shrugged. "Everythin' changed. They got so much junk now, they're set. The Barrow goin' anywhere's like a parade. People come out to meet 'em."

Missy's voice trailed off as they passed a sign. ABITIBI CANYON COLONY WELCOMES YOU. EST. 1930. Another sign had been nailed below it. It said, in a spraypaint scrawl, DO NOT ENTER. HAZMAT EXPLOSIVES POISONS TOXICS.

"Y'know…" He scratched his beard. "I think I 'member when Mick got that memo from the union. Sayin' they was gonna send out a rep tellin' us to do things different. Sounds borin' to sit through. Hoah! There you have it. Home sweet home."

KA-THUNK THUNK. At the crest of a hill the truck crossed an abandoned railway line and there lay the whole of Abitibi—an old hydro station straddling a fast-flowing river flanked by walkways and generators of crumbling cement. Beyond that were three parallel streets carved out of the forest, none of them leading anywhere except to each other. Some houses were boarded up, some not. Larger buildings, long and low, held signs crackled and weathered. The station and its single-purpose town of three hundred people in the middle of an ocean of woods had been shut down, all its doors closed one last time. Then everyone had left. For a long time Abitibi

Canyon and its hydro relic slept, forgotten until the Crummies remembered it.

In the middle of Second Street (there was also a First, and a Third, and that was all) a pack of idling flatbeds, log skidders, cubes, diggers, trailers, and hydraulic lifts pulled by the engines and cabs of one-ton trucks, sat idling. *It's not a ship,* Missy thought, remembering the driver's shrug, unclear to her until now. *It's a convoy.* Eli drove past slowly, calling out to figures she did not yet know. At the street's dead end he turned and approached the pack from its rear, pulling in between two trucks and turning the key in the ignition. The vibration underneath her stopped.

"This is it," he said. "Time for you to meet the lot. We're movin' out. Got a ways to go this week. There's a factory about to be demolished in Beaudry, across the Quebec border, and we wanna get there before non-union scrappers get the pick of it. Auto parts. Gonna be a haul o' good metal. We just gotta load up…"

Missy grasped the door handle and turned to him. "Thanks, Eli."

"Go hop on the bus and I'll see you. Straight to your first Crummy junk run, pretty much! Stay sharp, eh?"

"I will." She popped the door, landing neatly on the pavement. She swung her backpack over her shoulder as Eli's truck pulled away.

The bus. Which one's the bus?

There it was: the back of a yellow school bus hacked up and welded onto the front of a one-ton truck. A cough of blue smoke belched out the muffler and tangles of pirate limbs and heads burst out each out window as if under pressure from the inside. She took a deep breath and approached the cab through a tangle of weeds and roots.

"I'm—"

"Take yer pick, girl!" the driver barked. "We gots chopper crummies an' transport crummies and this one here—" She slapped the outside of the door with her hand. "This here's for thugs with rocks fer guts. You got rocks fer guts?"

"Yeah," said Missy. "I do."

"Then snap to it, girl!" The pirate she'd know as Gudie laid on the gas. The crummy swayed as the engine's lazy idle roared to attention and Missy stepped through the mud and onto the back step. The door sprang open and she swung herself up.

For a moment, a busload of hulks stared at her and she stared back. Then Gudie let out the clutch and the crummy lurched forward, pitching the small girl down the aisle in a tumble. A leg, propped out with a "Hup!," stopped her abruptly and she collected herself, looking up into a mouthful of black teeth.

"Romeo Marcoux, brute!" Missy could see that he yelled. "Union told us yeh don' hear good. YEH DON' HEAR GOOD."

A hand reached out from behind the brute and clapped the side of his head.

"Shoutin's not gonna do nothin'! *Vous smatte! En tout cas,*" he gestured at Missy. "*C'est flo*, she's got 'ere, *non*? She catch enough, 'owever she does it, don' matter." He turned to her, shaking his head good-naturedly.

"I'm Louis Smellie," he said. "Coxswain in charge of dat brute—" Romeo shrugged, grinning.

"...Dat one, Guillaume—" a stocky, curly-haired man with massive arms gave a salute ("GILLY!" the others cheered in unison).

"...An' Gudie drivin' up front, who you already met, she's a brute too. She's *pas de nom*, so we call her *La Sauvagess*."

"Savage?" Missy was adept enough at lip reading to make sense where lines between languages blurred.

"The very one! Nobody know where she come from. But everybody know she crazy-*tof*. Now, all youse! Interduct yerselfs."

A woman with two very tight braids moved over to make space. Missy nodded her thanks and sat down.

"Jean Erie, Navigator," she said. "You're a Dread? Me and Meena served our master class together. She's good stock."

A very greasy, dark-haired man in grey coveralls turned around from the bench seat in front of them.

"Tobias Murphy, Machinist." He pointed out the window. "Hup! And through the trees there ahead of us you can see the sloptruck, that's Winfield, he don't trust nobody else with the food..."

Missy peered through the window at a refrigerated cube van that lumbered along the edge of the clearcut. Another pirate, next to Tobias, turned in his seat.

"Luther Cree, First Mate."

The pirates exploded again with unintelligible cries of "LE CHEUF!" and Missy nodded respectfully in the presence of the crew's senior officer, a friendly, spare man with weathered skin and hair that hung straight much like hers.

"Hello, sir," said Missy. Luther waved away the formality.

"Ah, it's Luther or *Cheuf*, whatever you like. We don't get too formal 'round these parts. Where'd you just come from? London, eh?" He winked. "You're in high country now. You keep your feet under you and don't fuss about anything else."

A few more said hello, and hands slapped her on the back, and then the pirates turned to talk amongst themselves as the crummy lumbered along. For a while Missy and Jean sat companionably, Missy just absorbing it all, until she felt a tap on her knee.

"We're almost to the work site. You can see the rest of them." Jean gestured out the window, leaning back so that Missy could have a look, tapping for her attention when it came time to note names.

"There's Cyr Langlois, our winchmaster." A pair of giant legs stuck out from underneath the tail end of a modified tractor.

"Norah, she's the transport engineer. We call her Straps. And there—" She pointed further down the road. "Vernier Pichette drives the flatbed; he's got a load of railway ties. And Zaps Grandeau, she's our electrician, over there driving the supply truck. And…where'd he get to? Ah, there." She nodded toward a massive log transport, a sixteen-wheeler with high arms and a crane for lumber and, for the Crummies, the biggest and most unwieldy junk. "There's Sol Johnson drivin' the skidder. He's the lead chopper. And there's Captain with him, Ripsaw Mick MacKenzie."

The one in charge, as it always seemed, was big in every way that one in charge should be—in voice, temper, and footprint. Even from a ways back, as the Crummies' captain leapt down from the cab to land heavy on the ground, Missy was struck with the vision of a black bear dressed in denim and plaid, him and all his black-bear buddies driving trucks and yelling to each other through open windows. For these pirates were all kinds of furry and shaggy and brown, built like that, each of them a pile of bricks.

Chapter Five

IN THE DEEP OF ABITIBI

To: Eric. June 5.
Cyr and me had to go into town to get
supplies for a junk run
and GUESS WHAT he let
me drive the crummy
all the way down third street! I
need a spotter for a set of ears to: Eric Stewart
but that's OK. And they put P.O. Box 17
platforms on pedals. We're RR# 4
scrapping in Quebec and then New Germany, NS
heading up so high we'll BOR 1G0
almost be to the Inuit. I'm thinking if I had
to take algebra I'd run away to find some
pirates. Missy p.s. If you see the Barrow tell
Vince I got him some of those
moose gut banjo strings.

Parc
oméga
MONTEBELLO

CANADA 134

CERF DE VIRGINIE
WHITE-TAILED DEER

IMPRIMÉ / PRINTED IN CANADA

• • •

On day four, at dawn on the outskirts of Beaudry, Romeo
beckoned Missy through a cloud of exhaust and the girl stepped
forward. He tore a length of duct tape from the roll with one
hand and gave Missy a bundle of clothes with the other.

"Your firs"aul. Big day. Put this on. Then gimme yer arm."

Missy pulled the hooded shirt over her head. The brute tore off another length of duct tape.

"We count the seasons by the bites. 'Orseflies when it's 'ot and sunny. No bare skin. They take a chunk. Mosquitoes when it's damp, deerflies too. They both sting through yer clothes, though they have a tough time diggin' through ripstop."

Vernier, passing, knocked Missy with an elbow.

"*Au chalet de ma grand-mère, les maringouins sont tellement gros qu'ils doivent se mettre à genoux pour nous piquer dans le front!*"

Missy smiled at the accompanying charades, then looked to Romeo.

"'E says at his *grand-mère's*, the mosquitoes were so big they had to get down on their knees to bite him in the forehead. Bah. I seen 'em bigger than that in Chibougamou." Romeo nodded approvingly at the shirt that hung to Missy's knees. "The blackflies, we get them all year 'cept when the frost bites. They'll crawl under your sleeves and up your pants and into your ears. Head into the woods up here without the right stuff and you'll be a feast for all things."

Missy held out one arm, then the next, sleeves drooping well beyond her hands. Romeo rolled them up and wound the tape around her wrists to her skin. He handed Missy a bandana. She unfurled it. It was black with neon flames. The pirate grabbed it again and folded it, applying it to Missy's head over her ears and tying it snugly. He pulled the hood overtop, cinching the string tight around Missy's face. Finally, he wound a length of duct tape around the girl's neck and another around her waist. Romeo stood back, appraising his work.

"You look like a proper Crummy now." He nodded, pleased. "You are ready for the woods."

• • •

Day twenty-six of Missy's apprenticeship was one of those sunny ones with a bite to the wind, which there always was, even in early summer. Vernier, exasperated, turned with a wrench in his hand to look up at Cyr.

"Eh! *Va pèter dans le trèfle*," he spat.

Cyr turned to Missy, on her way to enter the transmission fluid inventory into Mick's logbook.

"'E tells me to go an' fart in *les* clover, 'e does! Dat's t'ird time dis week we gotta broken driveshaft. 'Appens, you know. But t'ree times? 'E's d'wheelright. Not d'wheelwrong! *Câlice!*"

The captain appeared as he always did, like a fox. Cyr startled.

"Go easy on him, Cyr. He gets his share o' driveshaft troubles. You busted a winch last week, eh?"

"Gah," Cyr replied. "Me an' *soeur-pet*, we's like a coupla ol' married fogies. If I don' get 'is goat, 'o will?"

"Fair enough." Mick grinned. "Listen, we need ratchet straps for the load up front…"

Cyr was already moving. "Ratchet straps, on the double! An' a fancy cocktail for Sir Wheelwrong!" A frustrated roar erupted from underneath the crummy. Cyr whooped and leapt over a river of mud to his errand.

"Sirpet?" Missy puzzled. Crummy French, a mangled mix of backwoods Franglais, was a jumble of lips.

"*Pet de soeur.* Nun's fart." Mick waved a hornet off his ear without a pause. "All the good slurs are church slurs. That one's church an' farts. No better."

The pirate captain chuckled at Missy's earnest attention and shook his head. "Airbrakes an' ditch winchin' an' two-tongued insults. You can go an' work in Ottawa after a stint wit' us. Chief's gonna be pleased."

With a playful wink, Mick licked two fingers and dragged them across one eyebrow and then the other, then straightened an imaginary tie before strutting off through the clearcut as though it were Parliament.

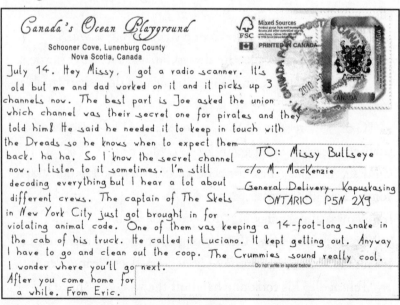

Canada's Ocean Playground

Schooner Cove, Lunenburg County
Nova Scotia, Canada

July 14. Hey Missy, I got a radio scanner. It's old but me and dad worked on it and it picks up 3 channels now. The best part is Joe asked the union which channel was their secret one for pirates and they told him? He said he needed it to keep in touch with the Dreads so he knows when to expect them back. ha ha. So I know the secret channel now. I listen to it sometimes. I'm still decoding everything but I hear a lot about different crews. The captain of The Skels in New York City just got brought in for violating animal code. One of them was keeping a 14-foot-long snake in the cab of his truck. He called it Luciano. It kept getting out. Anyway I have to go and clean out the coop. The Crummies sound really cool. I wonder where you'll go next. After you come home for a while. From Eric.

TO: Missy Bullseye
c/o M. MacKenzie
General Delivery, Kapuskasing
ONTARIO P5N 2X9

Do not write in space below

• • •

Day forty. The crummy rolled to a stop beside a Honda and was soon surrounded by respectable traffic at the red light. A green sign up ahead read KAPUSKASING, 12. Missy looked far below at the carful of teenagers, none of whom would blink twice at the sight of a beaten, mud-slathered truck. As far as any ordinary folk could see, these pirates were either tree planters or fellers venturing into town for supplies or rest, one side or the other in the scruffy, plaid, push and pull of the woods, of which Kapuskasing was the gathering place.

"You're about done, yeah?"

"Not quite." Missy felt a curious tug as the teens' car pulled away from the intersection, going straight while the crummy waited to turn left.

"You done well, y'know," he said. "Nice work the other day at the recyclin' plant. We wouldna found all that old cable unless you'd shimmied through that ducting, little garter snake."

He tugged uncomfortably at his shirt and sighed, easing the truck through the intersection. "I'll take frost over this any day. Can't see straight fer all the nibblin'. Not so bad, though, when you're covered in chassis grease. Nothin' like a good stink to throw off the blackflies."

"Right," said Missy. "Otherwise you wouldn't stink at all. It's just for bug protection."

"Tchaa!" Tobias took one hand off the wheel to shake his

fist in Missy's face, a fist that turned into a palm that rustled the top of her head. The crummy swayed a little.

Missy rested her head back, enjoying the breeze through the window as houses and stores flashed by. A sign in front of a junior high read REGISTER HERE FOR AUGUST DAY CAMP and she sank. *Almost time to be a spy.* Shame rose in her gut.

"Almost…" She had spoken aloud.

"August," Tobias said. "Got your next placement yet?"

Missy hesitated, looking long at the machinist.

"What is it, *flo?*"

"There's no more crews. I won't finish this year. This is it."

"What d'yeh mean, no more crews? What about… the Skels?"

"There's never an openin' with them. Everyone wants New York City."

"Oh, come on. The Cazas? Never met any of 'em but they've got the pick o' the Mediterranean."

"All booked up. People like the sun."

"The Excavas?"

"Stuck under a fault line in Ecuador."

"The Bombs?"

Missy glanced in the side mirror. "They're in refit."

He rattled off several more crews, incredulous that a useful pirate couldn't find a place, what with all the junk everywhere. She simply shook her head.

"You've got traffic on your tail, Tobias. Might want to pick it up."

The machinist drew air in through his teeth and laid on the gas. For a while he said nothing, his brow furrowed.

"It's too bad the…nah. They'd never… I doubt it." After a pause he turned to her. "There is another crew. They're not well thought-of, *flo*."

"I know." *He knows something*, she thought. The whirring vibration of studded tires on asphalt had made Missy numb. She shifted in her seat to face him, folding her legs underneath her, and he continued.

"Even if you could find 'em, union'd not honour it as a term. They're on black books. They might give you props just for the effort, if you could prove you'd spent some time with 'em… might count for something."

Or I could get them brought in…for my ship. Someday, my own ship. "Tell me more." She tensed.

Turning to face the road in the way that eases conversation for both driver and passenger, but conscious of the angle she needed to see his speaking, Tobias began.

"Their blademaster, Taro, was my mentor. He taught me everything anyone could ever know about metalwork. Hardly says a thing but you just watch."

Missy nodded. There were Dreads like that.

"It's been near-on six years since I seen any of 'em, but we stay in touch under radar. They got friends. People who know why they do what they do."

Missy was perplexed. "They're junk pirates who don't junk. What do they do?"

"What do you think?"

"They say the Griffs got a spell put on 'em by a bird-spirit." Missy picked flakes of mud off the laces of her boot. "They say the Griffs never want to land ever again."

He snorted. "Not far from the truth. They got a view from way up there, Missy, of bad things done to wild places. And they don't like what they see. An' so they do somethin' about it."

"What do they see?" Missy, like any child, knew of bad things done to wild places, but the scale of it escaped her.

"Crimes, they call it. They're militant about paperwork, maybe more than any of us, to th' point of bein' unnatural. It serves 'em well. They keep records of everything. Evidence, charts, pictures. Then they monkey-wrench."

"Monkey-wrench?" Missy leaned forward, fascinated.

"Sabotage. They drill metal rods into trees to make 'em uncuttable. They block factory waste pipes and chimneys. They take all the bolts out of heavy plant machinery, glue the locks shut at mine gates, jam conveyor belts. It works, but only for so long. It gets 'em mighty close to bein' grabbed by the RCMP is what it does. The union's not protecting 'em anymore. If they're caught by the police, they'll be thrown into the clink. The real one. They'll be wishin' for a job tendin' one o' them photocopy machines at union headquarters. 'Specially with what they're up to now. People been whisperin' about it. Some big pipeline that's goin' across all kinds of country. They're fightin' it."

"Sabotage…" Missy spoke the word aloud, to her own ears an underwater murmur.

ROADWORK AHEAD. On either side of the highway, a crew of brushcutters inched along, painstakingly clearing forest that had encroached onto the shoulder of the highway. Tobias pressed the brakes as the crummy entered a detour rimmed with bright orange cones, then joined a line of cars waiting while a bulldozer lumbered across the road with a load of mangled wood.

"They need your Barrow, yeah?"

The girl didn't answer. Tobias pulled his eyes from the road to look at her.

"Look, *flo*. I'm tellin' yeh this 'cause…well. I shouldn't. But you can see when people've got justice in their bones. Makes 'em tough to knock over. Rasmus Krook. He's like that. His crew is like that. You're like that. You steal some time with them, and you'll learn a thing or two and get Chief's attention at the same time. What kind of attention, I dunno. But what else are you gonna do?"

Missy swallowed the shame of misplaced trust. A man in a reflective vest spun a sign from STOP to SLOW and the crummy advanced as Tobias continued.

"The Griffs cause as much trouble as they can for companies that earn that trouble. They've got friends among us who understand. Silent backers. Even activists, non-pirate folk. Local people who make noise when noise is needed."

"Why don't they just tell everyone what they see? The union couldn't be mad at that. The government would do something."

The pirate shifted in his seat. *Kids*, he thought, sighing.

"…Wouldn't they?" She demanded it of him, the nearest adult.

"The capitalist belly, that great rumblin' thing." He evaded her. Sort of. He just didn't know how to explain. "We're here."

She'd been watching him so closely she hadn't noticed.

DOMINION STREET GAS & CONVENIENCE

"But Tobias." The driver's side door slammed shut behind him. "We're already full."

He spoke through the open window. "Follow me."

The bell rang as they pushed into the gas station. Tobias walked with broad steps to the magazines and newspapers and scanned them back and forth until he picked one up and thumbed through it. Missy twisted to read the underside of the cover. *THE FARMERS' ALMANAC*. It shrank to miniature proportions in his hands.

"Here it is. *Celeste Starr's Best Days Astrological Forecast*. Code for friends, so we'll know where they'll be. Just in case. Shivers Cleary, their navigator, writes it like a joke page so farmers won't take it serious."

Missy leaned over his shoulder and saw a simple chart bordered with moon and star insignias. "Best for pickling pike," she read aloud. "April 10th to the 15th."

"Pickled pike? Pike…" He rubbed his palms together as if to jog a memory. "Right. That's Cree Lake, high up, Saskatchewan. Landing beacon 14, if I 'member right. Thick woods. Big fish. They got a smoke shack up there."

"August 10th to the 19th: best for airing long underwear."

"Undies…" He paused. "Pretty sure that's wheatlands, outside Moose Jaw. Beacon 8."

"February 22nd to the 28th: best for tent camping." Missy giggled.

"Notikewin. That's Alberta. They take over a provincial park after the wardens chain off the main road. They stay there if they got big repairs and have to sit tight. Decent facilities, y'know. Nobody goes in there in the off-season."

Missy nodded, impressed. "Best for reprimanding disobedient bears: November 22nd to the 28th."

"Ah, bears. Way up north. Beacon 2. That's Enterprise, Northwest Territories. Cars an' buses an' truckers stop there on the way between Yellowknife to Hay River or Alberta. There's a small airport, too. Too small an' too far north for Transport Canada to fuss about too much. Good raidin' for parts."

Tobias ran his finger down the chart, muttering to himself. Missy turned to walk through the aisles of the shop, giving him quietness to decode. Chocolate bars with a sheen of dust. Plastic tubs of windshield-wiper fluid. Crossword puzzles, fan belts. Then the pirate waved to her as he pushed the door open with the other hand, an urgent look on his face. As they walked across the parking lot she ran ahead of him, turning back to watch him speak.

"August 2nd to the 4th. Best for making hay. Alberta grasslands. Beacon 29. Blackfoot land. It's one of their soddie camps, like the old pioneers used to have. Mossy cabins you can hardly tell from a little hill. If we hurry, we'll get you settled with 'em before they head off for Moose Jaw."

Missy shuddered, set to task.

Chapter Six

INTERCEPTION

Mick pulled off his work gloves and propped them on the edge of the fire in the middle of Third Street. They sizzled a little, steaming. He pulled a stool underneath him and reached for wood, tossing two logs into the rusted oil drum with a crash of sparks. Even Abitibi's summer nights were brisk, and no blackfly liked the smoke of a drum fire. Crummies soaked in it like a bath.

"Mick. I know we talked about this last night, but we oughta take her to the Griffs." Tobias sat down next to his captain and waved Missy over. "She should finish and get certified, or at least get some respect at HQ. It's a bit early but she's got enough credits from us. And if we keep her for that extra half-term like we's wanted, the northern logging route's gonna be snowed in by the time we try an' get her to their next landing."

Missy squirmed in place, watching the captain. Mick unbuttoned his flannel, peeling off the day's grime to his undershirt. He scratched at his neck.

"Can't wait for frost. I'm right chewed up and spat out." He appraised a line of angry welts on his arm, then sighed and looked up at his machinist. "Fair guess about the northern route, past another half-term. As for the Griffs, I'm less sure."

The new wood cracked and shot more sparks into the air. Missy looked at Tobias. *Your turn*, he mouthed.

"Captain." She stepped into the smoke and he turned to her. "I want to try."

"They won't have you. They want nothing of apprentices. They only run. And the union won't hear of it. They'll just be mad someone else found 'em before they did. And they'll be doubly mad that you let 'em go, even though you couldn't stop 'em otherwise. You'd only be an antagonist, girl. To everyone."

"Leave that to me," she replied. "I'll get on board one way or the other. I've done it before. I'll see it's documented like any other term. Then I'll take it to the union and make 'em stamp it."

"You can't make the union do anythin', girl." Mick replied, agitated, standing up and towering over her. "They'll hold you at fault for not exposin' them for pickup. They may even call you a conspirator. That a kid found 'em when they've been huntin' 'em for years? You could get yourself blacklisted just for the insult of it. An' it'll be my fault for lettin' you go."

Missy was silenced by the shame of all she couldn't reveal. *They won't blacklist me. They hired me. I am already an antagonist. Just not the kind you think.*

"Captain," called Luther, and those in the circle turned, as did Missy. He sat with his boots up on a log at the far side of the fire. "The policy. As long as she documents it—every hour,

every job—they've got to consider it. Remember? They was
gettin' on all of us about paperwork, and so they made it so
you can't get a workterm certified without it. An' the reverse
is true. They can't reject a documented term. There's no clause
that cancels out work done with a blacklisted crew, long as it's
signed off by that captain."

"He's right, Mick." Jean, pinning topographical charts to air
on a line she'd strung between two trees, paused with a handful
of clips. "Happened to me when the Cazas got in trouble,
middle of my third term. They had to accept my work, even
though the crew was on the bad books. I had all my papers."

The woods went silent again except for the red pops and
cracks inside the drum. The captain nodded, deep in thought.
Sol, who sat forward with his elbows on his knees, waved for
Missy's eye. She turned.

"What is it you want so bad, *flo*?" The storied chopper had a way
of asking questions that got past everything else. Others nodded
and turned to Missy, who gazed from one figure to the next, studies
in exertion and plaid. She chose the best truth she could.

"I'm here because I'm like my mother." It had come to her
almost without thinking. She felt it, but couldn't be sure she'd
said it aloud. "She never stayed still."

Missy stood up. Eyes followed her.

"I don't just want to be a pirate, and I'm a long way from
that. I want my own ship. Until I get probation I'm nothing
but a stowaway."

With all that made him Ripsaw now, Mick MacKenzie remembered being stationless. And how it felt to be hungry, as folk without station tend to be. The girl spoke clean. She stood that way too. He looked down at her from almost twice her height, and swore she looked him back in the eye as evenly as though she were seven feet tall.

The lights of a truck turned around the corner, illuminating the scene in a way that felt startlingly blue and mechanical in firelight. The truck stopped and the driver's door burst open. A pirate jumped out. It was Guillaume. He closed the door behind him and reached the captain in three steps.

"Mick," he panted. "We been called up. West, dis time. Union picked up on the federal scanner the gypsum mine in Steep Rock's bein' all broken up, *tout le kit*."

Everything shifted. Jean began unpinning her maps. Sol reached for his boots. The captain looked from the apprentice to his brute and back again.

"We pack camp tonight. Tobias—you have the Griffs' flight plan?"

Missy could hardly breathe.

"Checked it this morning." Tobias stepped forward. "They'll land at beacon 29 in less than a week."

Mick looked wryly at Missy. The camp was already in a state of dismantling, pirates gathering bits and odds of things, calls rousing the others to truck and trailer.

"For a stowaway with no station you've got nerve as well as

luck, girl. We'll turn north at Winnipeg. That gets you almost
there, with papers from us. A day's drive past that and we hit
the backyard of the Blackfoot. Practically on the way. I'll take
you. Long as you're ready to be unstill, that is."

"I'm ready, Captain." Missy steadied herself despite the
chief's words choosing this moment to invade her mind.

You are owned by me and me alone.

• • •

Small towns and campsites and dozes with heads lolling back,
filthy hands grabbing inside cardboard boxes for doughnut
holes passed back at drive-thrus, a blur of forest and then more
forest and the strip of pavement snaking around lakes, so many
lakes. Missy beat Romeo eight times in a row at rock-paper-
scissors, each time best two of three.

The pirates rolled into parking lots and rest stops alongside
bewildered tourist families in station wagons. It was a
bumper-to-bumper convoy of mud-encrusted monster tires
and jacked-up tractors and the sixteen-wheel log skidder
and its giant-implement cousins of break-apart, all of which
looked terribly ominous, amplified not only by the skulls and
crossbones here and there, on mudflaps and doors, but by the
characters that came tumbling out when the engines rattled
to halt. Giants wrapped in heavy-duty canvas and threadbare
hunter plaid, people so weathered they looked positively
coniferous, doused in sap and all things prickly. Ordinary folk
grasped preschoolers and held them close, but the north was

stacked abundantly with coniferous sorts, people of the woods. Just enough so that grasps loosened amid whispers of *It's okay, honey, they're just tree planters, they're a strange bunch,* or *I've heard the loggers are on strike, they must be all emptying from the cuts.*

Halfway through Manitoba, lakeland became grassland so abruptly that Missy felt they'd driven through a doorway from one national room into the next. She had never been this far west. She gazed out the window at some fields cropped short, some proud and tall. A railway ran parallel to the Trans-Canada, and an endless freight train crawled along beside the traffic before turning off for parts unknown. She watched it chug away into the flat distance for half an hour.

A playful shove on her arm and Missy turned in her seat to see the brute Romeo smiling, and the others too.

"What?" She smiled. "I didn't see."

"You got stars in yer eyes," he said, the crummy rumbling underneath them. "What, you never been outta Dread country?"

"Only the other way. Across the ocean. England. Never this way."

"Ah, there's a whole lotta west to be 'ad, *flo.*" He shoved past two rows to sit beside her. The seat heaved as he settled into it, and he gestured over her and out the window. "Dis is but the front porch o' the west. Dere's mountains wit' snow on top, an' places all jagged wit' names like Hell's Gate an' Desolation Sound an' the Broken Islands, an' you t'ink dis is prairie? You 'ave not seen prairie. Tall grasses like ocean. Space, so much space you'll want to run an' run an' never stop at the sight of it."

•••

They passed campervans and grocery store delivery trucks with gigantic hamburgers painted on the sides and airport shuttles full of people in suits and ties. At rest stops Missy would hop from truck to truck for a change of space and company. She climbed up into the skidder cab with Vernier, who loved Carl Perkins ("King o' Rockabilly, girl!"). He'd sing along, loud, Missy seeing volume rather than hearing it, mute comedy.

I'm an ol' poor boy, long way from 'ome

He belted out, sweeping one hand, the other on the wheel, axles wobbling in time.

I'm an ol' poor boy, long way from 'ome
Guess I'll never be happy, everythin' I do is wrong, yeah!
She sang along too.

•••

"Any mine's a gold mine."

At a gas station in Falcon Lake, Missy climbed up into the cab of the flatbed truck between Louis, who drove, and Gudie, who said very little. They rumbled in the middle of the pack, 4x4 tires knobbling and bucking on unnatural pavement.

"Good metal, heavy machinery, scrap…"

Dismantlings on this scale only came around once every couple of years, a window of opportunity as brief as it was rare. Spirits were high.

"…trailers, ties and rails…they shut the gates after the last worker leaves on a Friday and then they switch on the security cameras…"

Gudie, all dark eyes and wordlessness, nudged for Missy's attention and patted the electrical wire cutters she kept leashed to her pocket.

"…An' then we got until Monday at dawn to pick the place clean. That's when the government cleanup crew arrives. They get there to a busted padlock and their job already done for 'em."

A green sign said JUNCTION #6 HIGHWAY 2 KMS.

"Heads up," he said. "Highway 6. We go north. You go west."

•••

"You're solid, Bullseye." Mick looked at her as he pulled away from the rest stop, following the convoy, gravel spitting out from under them, one by one. He would take Missy as far as he could, and meet up with his crew later, on the take. "Yeh learn quick. An' it seems yer always thinkin', a step ahead of where we are."

Missy shrugged. "I keep an eye on what I can."

"You do," Mick replied. In front of them trucks and flatbeds and the bus slowed, easing off the highway bound for the mine. As Mick's truck passed the ramp there were waves and fists in the air and faces against glass and Missy watched them fondly, a last goodbye. They were alone on the highway now.

"Listen, Missy," he said. "There's somethin' you got to know. About the Griffs. Murphy told you some, yeah?"

She nodded.

"What they do, Missy…it's against the law."

"What *you* do is against the law."

"Yeah, but it's different." He shifted in his seat. "We got the union PR an' workarounds an' payoffs. They don't. Soon as they gave up junkin', they gave up protection. Every time they set out to wrench, they come close to gettin' hauled away by the RCMP. To jail, Missy. Real jail. Locked up so deep there's nothin' the union could do for 'em, even if they was inclined, which they're not."

Missy was silent.

"Listen up, girl." He turned as much to her as he could with his eyes still on the road. "You get any sense o' badness, of them gettin' caught, of someone catchin' up to 'em—you promise me you'll run."

"That's against pirate code," Missy said softly. "You don't run if your crew doesn't run."

"Bugger the code. They opted out. You didn't. I get what they do and why they do it, but look after yerself first. Promise me."

"I promise." Missy looked at the floor. He nudged her, demanding her to say it to his face as she needed him to do the same. "I promise, Mick."

It was Missy's fifty-second and final day with the

Crummies. The sunset cast a warm glow into the cab of the truck, due west.

•••

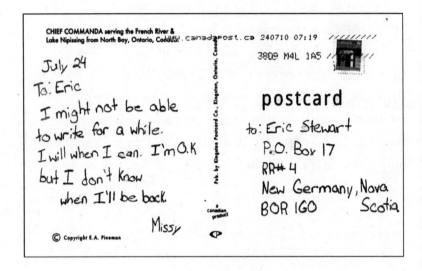

CHIEF COMMANDA serving the French River &
Lake Nipissing from North Bay, Ontario, Canada

.canadapost.ca 240710 07:19 ////////
38D9 M4L 1A5 //

July 24
To: Eric
I might not be able
to write for a while.
I will when I can. I'm O.K
but I don't know
    when I'll be back.
                Missy

© Copyright E.A. Pineman

Pub. by Kingston Postcard Co., Kingston, Ontario, Canada

canadian
product

postcard

to: Eric Stewart
P.O. Box 17
RR# 4
New Germany, Nova
BOR 1GO   Scotia

Chapter Seven

THE HEARING OF LITTLE PIKSII

A fragrant, grassy freshness lived here alongside the musty infirmity of age. In the darkness, these mingling scents were a welcoming presence. Missy shook her head. *No,* she whispered from the doorway of this home made of earth, crossing the threshold a spy. *I am unwelcome. You just don't know it yet.*

Ripsaw Mick had pulled away with more stern warnings, making sure to see her settled and stocked. *Use the radio, girl,* he'd said. *Tell us what you see. A whiff o' trouble, or they don't show up—we'll come for yeh.* Then he was gone down the highway to catch up with his crew.

The wind swept hair into her face as she fumbled behind her hand with a match. The stick ignited, a small but significant whoosh of life. Touched to the wick of the lantern and then sheltered under glass, the flame steadied, undisturbed by the wildness of the prairie, illuminating her immediate vicinity. She scrambled to her feet and lifted all her belongings inside one by one: her backpack; the canvas duffle filled with Crummy offerings to the Griffons, should she find them; a plastic folder containing instructions from Tobias; and a letter from Mick to

the Griffons' captain testifying to Missy's intentions. She shut
the heavy wooden door behind her, muffling shelter from the
outside.

With the lantern held at arm's length, the edges of the
soddie's interior came into focus. There were plain mats on the
floor, sturdy long tables, and a massive fireplace along one wall
hung with cast-iron pots and implements. A door at the back of
the room led to sleeping quarters, small rooms with bunks, and
a supply shed joined on the side. The homes of mice and insects
and small snakes had been uprooted when the wall was formed,
however many generations ago, and the creatures had stayed.
Every now and then, one would skitter companionably. *Water
must find a way in when it rains*, she thought. She was right.

Around the back of the soddie was a lean-to filled with
wood. She carried an armful inside, kindling piled on top, and
lit a small fire—not for heat, but to fend off the damp and keep
her company. It crackled and popped happily. She opened the
provisions bag Winfield had given to her, laying everything
on the table—food for one, several days' worth dwarfed by
its setting. Jam cookies and hard tack and canned stew and
powdered milk and porridge, and a pile of what Winfield
lovingly called "moose poops"—squashed dates rolled up and
baked with whatever porridge hadn't been eaten the day (or
week) before. She swept kindling splinters and bark off her
sweater and stood in the middle of the soddie, satisfied.

"I'm ready," she spoke aloud. She put another log on and

dug in her bag for the briefing she'd kept secretly stowed since that day at headquarters. Memos, chronological histories, maps, diagrams. She stretched out on a thick braided rug in front of the fire, belly-down, and laid the papers out in front of her.

```
BACKGROUND
CREW: The Griffons
TRANSPORT: Hercules freight aircraft body Gunnar II [1]
modified w/helicopter rotors [4]
Captain. . . . . . . . . Rasmus Krook
First Mate / Co-Pilot   Finola Prince
Engineer .. . . . . .. . Magnus DUTCH Molsson
Coxswain .. . . . . .. . Rolf THE WOLF Jaeger
Brute. . . . . . .. . . . TWO-HANDS Ginsberg
Brute. . .. . . . . . . . Billy Grundy
Metalsmith. . . . . .. . Birdie Worthy
Machinist.. . . . . .. . Cirrus Worthy
Greensmith. . . . . .. . Philippa PIPP McInnes
Navigator.. . . . . . . . Siobhan SHIVERS Cleary
Windmaster. . . . . .. . Cam Falconer
Bladesmith. . . . . .. . Taro CAT Takeshi
Wireman. .. . . . .. . . Brock Jones
Aerologist. . . . . .. . Gwynne Wickliff
Junior Aerologist. .. . Jesper JAILBIRD Göransson
```

HISTORY:

The Griffons last reported for remittance at the depot in Thunder Bay on April 14, 2002. They have not had union contact since. Repeated attempts to locate them by officials have failed due to the nature of their airborne transport. Several unconfirmed sightings indicate the crew may still be active and in flight, their purpose unknown.

REGION: North American Midwest/Prairies

SHIP DESIGN:

The *Gunnar II* is comprised of the fuselage of a Hercules freight plane modified with small wings and four tilt rotors for the vertical lift of a helicopter plus the speed and range of a conventional fixed-wing aircraft. Before its disappearance, the *Gunnar II* had been inventoried as follows:

- Max cruising speed 571 km/h
- Wing span 40.41 m (132ft 7in)
- Length 34.37m (112ft 9in), height 11.66m (38ft 3in)
- Max payload 23,158kg (51,054lb)

DELINQUENCY: Continued failure to report

STATUS: Outstanding warrant. Blacklisted.

Missy tried to imagine travelling a thousand kilometres in two hours. She could not. *Eleven metres high? That's big. Carrying 51,000 pounds of what, if not junk?*

A red light flashed in the corner of her eye and she leapt to her feet.

("Bullseye, Bullseye," a voice called out. "Come in, Bullseye."

And then another voice. "Yeh can't talk into it, she's not 'earin' you!"

"Well fer crap's sake, what now? Why she got a radio?")

She made her way across the room and picked up the small black box. It vibrated. Someone was talking. She pressed the button.

"I can't hear you, whoever it is! Good lord, you guys are thick."

The light went red again as some Crummy or another pressed to speak.

("Sorry, Missy!"

"*Vouz avez des bébites dans la tête!* Stop talkin'! Let 'er signal us back, eh?")

The light went dark again and Missy knew this to be her turn. She pushed the button.

"I can't hear you, but I can talk fine. No sign of any Griffons yet, but I got lots of food, tell Winfield thanks. An' there's wood for the fire. So—"

She didn't know what else to say.

"—I'll stay put. I'll call you if I need to. Hey—how long are you from being done with the mine?"

("Cheuf say we gotta be outta here in two d—OW!"

"*Imbécile!* Push the button for the days!")

Missy felt yelling through her fingers. The button went dark, and then lit. Then it flashed one more time. *One—two.* If the Griffons didn't show up soon, she'd have to radio for a pickup on the Crummies' way by.

"Got it," she replied. "Two days. 'Night, Crummies."

"*BON SOIR!*" a voice yelled, a vibration that shook the radio enough to almost make her drop it. She grinned and pressed the button one more time.

"Watch out for that bum forklift, Romeo. Thing's gone all pitchy and with a load the weight'll buck you right off."

A thousand miles north, in a trailer next to an overturned forklift, a pirate with a mud-encrusted face gaped at another who laughed at his expense.

"'Ow'd she know dat? 'Ow?"

•••

Blacklisted

The fire was almost out, down to embers. She watched it fade.

Blacklisted

She wondered if they'd be giants. She was most familiar with giants.

Blacklisted

Her eyes fluttered closed and she wondered nothing else.

•••

Within moments of waking she had rekindled the fire, fetched water from the cistern, and taken a steaming mug of oatmeal

out to see the morning. She moved into the grass for another
look at where she was. A house of earth, but with windows and
a chimney. *They got them soddie camps everywhere,* Tobias had
explained. *One at every beacon. Sometimes one cabin, sometimes
more. They just look like earth, 'cause that's what they are. But they're
tidy, long as you don' mind the snakes...*

From the outside it looked like it had grown up out of the
ground, but from the inside, like it had dropped from the sky
complete with mugs and rugs and logs for the fire. To the west,
a distant wall of mountains rose from the flatness of the prairie
as though they stood watch over it. A three-legged signal pole
stood beyond the cabin like a lighthouse in an ocean of high
grass. At the very top of it was a solar bulb, its eye shut in the
daylight, anchoring a white panel stencilled in black with "29"
and one neat G.

I am in the right place.

•••

Later that evening, she looked up from her book. She wasn't
sure why. It was as though the air had changed, a second
heartbeat within her body. *Thump thump thump, thump thump
thump.* She stood for a moment—almost listening—staring at
the little black box, a straight line to friends. It was dark.

She dampened the fire, covering any trace of herself. She
found her boots, laced them, and stepped outside, pulling the
door shut behind her. *Thump thump thump.* Lights in the sky
illuminated the exhaust of gathering cars, and there was the

distant scent of a barbeque. She was not alone after all. *A town, so close?* She'd never have known it. The prairie rose and sank here and there almost imperceptibly, and the soddie camp lay in a low spot, enough to put the far distance over the crest of the flattest of all hills. Her stomach growled, tired of crackers and tuna from the can. She began to run and within three rolling fields she saw it: an arbour, open-air and glowing golden, pulling crowds of people into it. She remembered Tobias's description of beacon 29. *Blackfoot land.*

The sound, though it shocked her to think of it that way, became more resonant as she approached. She crept towards the structure on its dark side, behind the stage, and flattened herself against pounding wood, inching along until she found an opening and looked through.

Just above where she stood, children ran along the encircling bleachers trailing ribbons and playing tag. A canteen sent a column of delicious smoke into the air, and a long lineup streamed away from it with plates of meat and bread. People laughed and embraced. Dancers walked among the crowd, winged eagles and quilled porcupines and women in dresses that jingled as they walked, the fringes of their shawls bright with colour. In the centre of it all was the grassy circle that had glowed so bright. Nearby, their backs to her, a dozen men sat shoulder-to-shoulder around the biggest drum she'd ever seen.

She squeezed through the opening and underneath a few rows of bleachers to hover near the drum, entranced. The men spoke among themselves, focused, tightening hides for the next song. The one closest to her sensed her and turned, resting his drumstick on his knee.

"Hey, little *piksii*. You should go somewhere else. It's going to get loud here."

Missy found the only words she felt. "Loud is good."

Lou looked curiously at the girl who had appeared out of nowhere. It was a solemn thing, to drum. It was no spectacle for gawkers with white sneakers and throwaway cameras. But she was unusually still for her age, this girl with the wide eyes. He gestured for her to do as she liked. She came closer and knelt in the dirt, folding herself into inconspicuousness. The lead drummer summoned the song and Lou's voice joined in, as did the others, and together the men lifted their drumsticks high into the air. Then they met rawhide with a crack.

Missy jumped. Her insides were like particles of dust atop the drum, vibrating with every beat. She pressed her hand against the rounded wood: *I can hear it. I can hear it!* The beat intensified, calling the dancers, and Lou's fringe shook against her shoulder as he drummed and sang.

This could never, ever be too loud.

Then she was on her feet, approaching the inner circle of dancers. Lou hesitated, almost losing his place. It wasn't proper. Others noticed too, pointing, but then she was already out there, swallowed up by a host of eagles who pounded the earth around her, bustles circling and looping through the air to the beat of the drums. Jingle dancers stepped in time, their faces flushed. One crew in porcupine roaches and another in buffalo-bone breastplates joined in from the far side of the circle and the crowd of dancers grew and grew, swirling together like a school of mackerel in the ocean currents of Missy's east. She had stumbled her way to the centre through a blur of colour and movement. The girl who seemed to belong to nobody spun and stamped the earth, following the song as it throbbed through her body, her very heart jammed up inside her throat.

She bumped into some dancers who glanced at her disinterestedly, absorbed in the concentration and sweat of it all. Others smiled, took her hand, or brought her in line with rows of feathers and beadwork, showing her unfamiliar steps. She said very little—even less than usual—but her eyes were a kaleidoscope, and she earned a place of sorts. Lou, feeling responsible, had kept an eye out from his place at the drum. He could see well enough that the night had moved her in a way he didn't yet understand.

She stayed all night. She ate richly, juice on her fingers, and ran and tussled with boys and girls who called themselves Bloods, a tribe within the Blackfoot nation. At a quarter to midnight she stood again on the dark side of the arbour, the drummer Lou sending her off through lingering woodsmoke.

"You sure you don't need a hand back to the beacon?"

In his watching of her throughout the night, it had occurred to him who she must belong to.

She startled. "Beacon?"

"You're on my land. I know who you are," he said. Behind him the wooden building glowed, an oasis. "Maybe not who you are, but *what* you are."

She looked back at him in silence, unsure of what to say.

"We are friends." He turned up toward the sky, searching, then lowered his face back to her. "We take care of things when they're not here. I can walk with you, if you want. It's late."

Missy shivered a little, fidgeting. "I can manage on my own."

She turned in the direction of the camp. He reached out to her shoulder, turning her to speak as he now knew he must.

"You liked our drum, little bird. Our grandfather's spirit is in there, inside that drum. He calls to those who are strong."

"I know. I heard," Missy, her hands on her hips, struck a posture of capability and wonder. Then she turned in grass that reached her shoulders, and with a flash of blue fringe that someone had braided into her hair, she was gone.

Lou stood for a while, gazing out into the night toward the refuge of his friends. Pete, a fellow drummer, appeared at his side.

"That girl is with the night-walker."

Lou nodded. "She is, or she will be."

"Do you think she knows what she's in for?" They turned together toward the light.

"No, Pete." Lou shook his head. "I don't."

Chapter Eight

THE GIRL WITH THE PLENTY OF MEANS

BANK 20 DEGREES TO STARBOARD

CLOUD COVER DIMINISHING

We make earth. The captain rose and the thrum changed tone. Around him was a flurry of bodies knocking, gripping, strapping down. Ritual. Another voice.

ALTIMETRE IS 29.50 INCHES MERCURY

PICKING UP BEACON 2-NINER DELTA ECHO

He looked out the portside window. Despite the impenetrably grey sky, Rasmus knew where he was—among tall grasses that would soon be whipped into frenzy by the blades at his command. Among friends.

WINDS 14 KNOTS NORTHWEST

"Captain," said another voice, this one at his shoulder. "We are clear to land."

He nodded, and his nod was passed to the cockpit, and he joined his crew as the Griffons began to descend.

•••

Low clouds made everything on the earth crouch. Pressing the grass down with a thick rug she'd found, Missy lay stretched out on her back, watching the sky.

It has to be today. She was a patient sort, but a realist, too. If something didn't happen soon, she'd have to signal the Crummies to come for her. Much longer and she'd miss them on their way back through. Then it would be weeks. Back east, the chief was already waiting.

As she shifted to sit cross-legged for hard tack and warm milk, a pack of foxes unaware of her presence slinked by, sauntering and sniffing until one of them looked up, alarmed. They scattered, darting into hiding. Missy set her mug down. The hair on her arms stood up. Then she saw what the foxes had heard: a churning sky, a hole forming as though someone had plunged a handheld blender into liquid. She jumped to her feet.

Here they come.

From inside the column there shot a jet of cloud and the ship appeared. She ran into the field, away from the soddie, to where it might land. It descended a while, growing in size as it approached, stirring the air until she felt almost lifted off her feet. It was light grey with a massive girth and four rotor props, both a helicopter and a plane. It was the biggest thing she'd ever seen, like five Barrows put together in flight. It was upon her now, and the air around her whipped her hair and tugged at her clothes. She couldn't hear the *whop-whop-whop* exactly, but it reverberated against her. Dust and dirt pelted her face. She blinked to clear it.

They've seen me. She raised one hand, her palm facing out in a gesture of good intention. A lie. She took steps back instinctively as the ship hovered for landing, its nose pointed directly at her. The wind of it was so intense now that she had to turn away, her arm shielding her face. Then it touched ground, the rotors slowed, and in the softness of a summer morning, over grass still wet with dew, she approached.

•••

"Captain. Someone is there," his pilot spoke into the headset. "Just one, a person with no means."

"*Ner på marken*," he said sternly. "To the ground. This someone has not only seen us, but expects us, which would indicate plenty of means."

He turned and left the cockpit to brief the crew and have the stern door unsealed. The pilot pulled back on the throttle, her eyes fixed on what she now saw was a young girl, her hand outstretched in greeting.

No one like this should know us to greet us. But it would seem she does.

A spongy impact rocked the ship as wheels made ground.

•••

Rotor blades slipped through the air above, winding down, and the tall grasses of the prairie settled themselves into their calm sway once more. Without the aggression of flight the ship exhaled, a tired whirr that registered through Missy's body as a white noise. Then movement: a loading ramp at the tail slowly opened. She ran to meet it but stood a ways back, still uncertain of what would come out of the metal gloom.

A large man with stringy hair and burnished skin appeared. He wore high boots and flight goggles, and coveralls smeared with black grease. He paused at the top of the ramp before walking slowly to the ground.

"Who are you?"

"I am an apprentice," Missy replied. "Who are you?"

He pushed the goggles up onto his forehead, pale blue eyes fixed on her.

"We are not in need of an apprentice."

Missy looked around him for any other signs of life from inside the ship. There were none.

"You are trespassing." He looked to the beacon. "And you've come a long way to do so."

She nodded. "I'm Missy. Missy Bullseye. Friend of the Crummies."

He hesitated, looking at the small girl inquisitively. Then he turned to the ship for permission, a signal. Someone else was listening. He turned to her again, resolved. The girl had found them, knew them. The chance for evasion had passed.

"I am Magnus Molsson. Flight engineer with the Griffons. Friends call me Dutch." He reached out to shake her hand. "Mick MacKenzie calls me Dutch."

A slight woman with a thick canvas jacket and the reddest hair she'd ever seen, near-dreaded, joined the engineer.

"This is Shivers Cleary, our navigator," said Dutch. *Best days*, thought Missy, remembering the almanac. The woman who'd written "reprimand disobedient bears" did not smile. More figures appeared from the shadows within the ship. A black-eyed man with a twisted beard walked down the ramp and came closer to her than anyone.

"Rolf, coxswain." Another man joined him, this one thick-necked and bald. He stared at Missy. Rolf broke the silence. "This is Ginsberg. Two-Hands. Brute."

A small, neat woman in a light-grey coat strapped tight stopped short at the bay door. "Gwynne Wickliff, aerologist."

A man with long black hair and a long black beard, staying back with the aerologist, nodded briskly. "I am Taro Takeshi. Bladesmith."

Many more emerged now, two and three at a time, filling the ramp.

"Finola Prince, first mate and pilot."

"Billy Grundy."

"He's a brute. I'm Cam Falconer. Windmaster."

"I'm Cirrus Worthy. This is my sister Birdie. We work with metal."

More followed, a blur of names and ship positions that were unfamiliar to her. Some looked at her with suspicion, and others with interest. Then the captain walked down the ramp. She knew it well enough before he spoke.

He was not a tall man, but he was tall enough. Coarse curls the colour of honey stuck out from underneath a small cap. His face was wind-blown, taut and baked. He also wore high boots, everything about him reined in. There was an unexpected sophistication to these men and women, a cultivated air that felt nothing like the woodsy roughness inside the gut of the Barrow. The crowd parted and he stood before her, his eyes alight.

"My name is Rasmus Krook. I am the captain."

"I am Missy Bullseye. Your apprentice."

He looked at her shrewdly. "You heard my engineer. We need no apprentice. We called for no apprentice. We deserve no apprentice, by the reckoning of some. Yet here you are, *helt plötsligt*."

She retrieved Mick's letter from her pocket and held it outstretched in her hand. "The Crummies told me you would be here."

He glanced at the endorsement of his old comrade's signature.

"I am useful, but I need probation," Missy continued. "I want my own ship someday and without you, I can't get it."

The engineer stepped forward again. "The union wants nothing but to lock us up. They'll not take our report of you no matter how useful you are."

"The union will hear the report of anyone who finds the Griffons. They been lookin' for you for years with no sign. They'll see I've earned it. All I need is a term, and then proof. Then I'll go on my way and leave you to…whatever you do. All I need is a few weeks, and then his signature." She pointed at the captain.

Rasmus Krook was quiet a while before he spoke again. The clouds moved fast overhead as a high wind picked up.

"You seek the signature of a pirate captain. We are not pirates. Not anymore. We are phantoms. We are kin to the great Gunnar, our famed *Spökis*, the greatest ghost pilot who ever was. We bow to no one but *örnen*, and *örnen* bows back."

Missy stood still. These were words she wasn't used to seeing, and lips forming them were a jumble. The black-eyed man with the twisted beard stood behind the captain's shoulder.

EAGLE, he mouthed, assuming a shortfall of language as opposed to a shortfall of hearing. She nodded a thanks only perceptible to her translator, and spoke again.

"I know you don't hunt for junk. But I know you are still pirates…" She gestured. "Look at you."

He glared at this unwelcome visitor. Then his face broke into a dazzling smile that filled his face with teeth, laugh lines, and dimples.

"Fair enough, young *flicka*."

"You call me *flicka*. I see it but I don't hear it, and you need to know that. It doesn't change what I can do."

"You are deaf to Swedish? Or to everything?"

"Both," she said, clenching.

He moved to stand directly in front of her, his face to hers.

"We have friends among unionists. Mick MacKenzie is one of them. This grants you consideration."

She nodded solemnly. "Yes, Captain."

He shook his head, amused at her presumption. "*Flicka* is 'girl.' You are useful, girl?"

"Yes," she replied.

"Our mission is not to be toyed with. You must be fortified to keep this company. Are you fortified, *flicka lilla*?"

Missy's eyes drifted to consider the crew one by one, and then travelled over the length and enormous height of their ship. Where the union's *Gunnar II* might once have been painted along the side, there was now another name. Boldly self-declared, the ship of the Griffons was the AVENGER.

"You don't weld like the others." She stepped through the grass and pressed her hand against a seam of metal, an abrupt chill against her palm. "Titanium alloy, right? Gas tungsten arc? One time I saw the Crummies weld a bulldozer to a trailer cab in eight minutes flat. They're metal butchers. The Blitzes aren't much more careful, either, although I'd bet their stuff's the strongest anywhere. But this…"

Reaching as high as she could, she traced the inner corner of a joint on the belly of the fuselage. "This is delicate work. Takes a steady hand."

A body snaked through the crowd to stand in front of her.

She was a head taller than Missy but slight and with golden skin, black hair cropped almost to her skull. She beamed, and in a single expression claimed her art.

"Yours?" Missy gestured to steel. "Birdie, right?"

The girl nodded. "Metalsmith."

Tugging at the fingers of each glove, the captain bared his hand and reached out.

"*Valkommen*. You are aboard."

• • •

"She…what?"

Eric stared dumbly at the blue scrawl in front of him, stamped and dated. He read it again. *Don't know when I'll be back.*

The goats, restless before a forecasted hurricane, bleated cantankerously in the pen underneath the attic window. A loose barn gate slammed repeatedly. He looked up at the chalkboard that held the month's schedule (an idea of Joe's, much to Hector's amusement): depot drops, mechanical upgrades, ship maintenance, community trips, ventures abroad. BULLSEYE was written, white against black, in the block for next week.

"Eric! Can you do the woodpile?"

He moved to the window and leaned out. His father, a kid goat under each arm, was on his way to the barn.

"I need you to strap down all the tarps. Once I get the animals tucked in I'm going to lock up. Can you make sure the hens are in the coop before the wind hits?"

He nodded before pulling the window shut, looking down again at the postcard in his hand. He turned it over. A cartoon beaver wearing sneakers and a Canadian flag bowtie held a sign that said I (HEART) NORTH BAY. He dropped it on the table and left.

• • •

But she is not with us.

    She is from a unionist crew.

Missy stepped onto the ramp and walked gingerly through a gauntlet of pirates who cast glances at her, some speaking in a hushed manner to one another as she passed.

"Griffons, to camp," called their captain. The gauntlet dissolved as individuals began a post-landing routine of inventory, offloading, and preparation of the soddie camp.

"This way, *flicka*. Follow me." The captain strode purposefully through the ship, urging Missy forward, and it was with his permission that she boarded the Avenger for the very first time.

"The freight hold." He gestured broadly. Pallets held square vats with spigots lined up in dated rows. As they walked they passed Dutch, who stood with a clipboard, counting.

"Our junk, our treasure." He patted a spigot approvingly as he passed.

"Junk?" Missy asked.

He turned to face her. "We make what we need. You will see. Now—crew quarters. We call it the mess."

He turned to grasp a ladder, climbed up through a hole, and she followed. Quilts were tacked up along the inside of the hull and thick rugs lined the floor, all buffering the metal.

"Insulation makes the most of what warm air we can muster," said the captain as Missy ran her hands across the softened wall. Daylight streamed in through portholes. A long table was flanked on one side by an open kitchen and on the other by a massive wall of cork that held a huge array of charts, maps, and photographs. Stacked hammocks lined the length of the fuselage. Everything in the room was battened down for flight, thoughtfully placed and cared for.

"This is no Barrow," she said softly, more to herself than to him. The captain chuckled.

"Hector Gristle...a fine captain. Haven't seen him in a decade or more..." He trailed off.

Blacklisted.

His face darkened, a rare expression of regret. Missy wondered what exile felt like.

Blacklisted.

"The Dreads are my home crew," she said. He nodded, and the moment passed.

"The lab, now. Keep up."

At the end of the mess there was another ladder, this time going down once more to the first level. Missy followed the Captain and emerged through a sheet of plastic and into a bright white room. Tubes and clear plastic plumbing covered every square inch, a brewery. A wall of books lined one wall, with a broad, stainless-steel counter on the other side. Computer consoles were mounted and plugged in, wires lashed together. Strapped neatly underneath the counter were an uncountable number of large bottles, all sealed and marked. Chemicals, powders, elements. Gwynne, the lead aerologist, turned with an armful of beakers. She had the brightest eyes Missy had ever seen.

"Welcome to my playroom." She winked.

Missy opened her mouth but nothing came out, her head on a swivel.

"Forward, forward…" Rasmus Krook urged her. "To the cockpit."

He led her through another doorway and into what seemed to be his quarters, a small meeting room of sorts with a map station and a brilliant spread of windows that formed the nose of the ship. From here, he could see everything. *Eagle eyes*, she thought. Once again she followed him up a ladder and through to the second level, to the highest and most revered seat of the aircraft. A landing at the top overlooked two pilots' chairs and a stunning mechanical array. Every inch of wall, ceiling, and floor was covered in buttons, switches, radar screens, indicator lights, pedals, thrusters, throttles, and keypads. Finola, first mate and pilot, turned in her seat with a small console in her lap.

"After we land, Fin records our mileage, notes the wind direction, tests every system," explained the captain. The pilot raised one finger, mouthing a count. "Fin is our very own *Spökis*.

In her fastidiousness she holds the fate of all of us. We must not interrupt her."

Missy followed the captain back down the steps, through the lab, and into the mess.

"What is a *spökis*?" she said. There was a movement from within the shadows of the galley. It was Jesper, Gwynne's assistant, the one they called Jailbird, stepping into the light eagerly as though he'd been waiting for the chance.

"*Spökis* was a rescue pilot in the Swedish mountains. They called him The Ghost because nobody ever saw him—he'd go up in the worst weather. People would only hear the sound of his engine. He'd fly when nobody else would."

Pirates filtered through, carrying loads and disembarking. The captain clapped his hands together and raised both palms.

"Altitude is risk, risk is vigor, vigor is life. Life is good!"

"LIFE IS GOOD!" Pirates in the vicinity shouted in echo, but she did not see, fixed on the pirate captain who stood in the middle of it all looking back at her with a knowing in his eyes. She swayed on her feet, not yet airborne but overwhelmed to the point of imbalance.

Chapter Nine

WHALE IN THE SKY

"Drink this." Pip was firm, her feet in a habitually wide stance to counter the pitching and rolling of the airship. She was the slopjack, though here, they did not call her that. Aboard the Avenger she was the greensmith, more guerilla botanist than baker or cook. She handed Missy a steaming mug.

You are low, flicka. The captain had guided her to the galley bench before returning to oversee duties in the hold. *It's been days, yes? Sleep evades those who wait. Pip will look after you. Stay with her for now.*

Missy blew across the top of the mug and a fragrant cloud curled back to envelop her face.

"Saskatoon berry." Pip nodded briskly. "Drink."

Missy obliged. It was hot and a little sour. The older woman eyed her approvingly.

"We steam, mash, and dry to never-ending bricks. Light and infinite." She reached into a compartment and withdrew a small, burnt-red hunk, displaying it in her palm. Missy sipped again.

"I chip pieces off as we need it. For stew, or boiled and added to bannock. Your tea is the leaves and the fruit. I steep it for two days." She gestured to the cast-iron kettle, which steamed with constant heat. "We use the inner bark and roots to treat pains. A miracle, this." She placed the brick back among a stack of others. "Drink."

The mug had cooled slightly, enough to afford her a cautious gulp, and Missy shuddered a little with the tartness.

"This berry…" Pip held one up, as small as a dried pea, and regarded it thoughtfully. In front of the porthole, she wore a halo of light. "This berry is our penicillin and our pancake."

Missy stared, feeling distant and groggy.

"Drink," Pip commanded. She did.

One more sip after that and Missy went limp, the inside of the galley turning sideways as she slumped. Arms lifted her into a soft place and tucked a thick cocooning blanket around her.

"You'll need your wits. But first, rest."

The greensmith's soothing went unheard by Missy's closed eyes, but the kindness released into the air made the girl submit to sleep. Days upon days she'd crouched in the soddie, hardly blinking for watching the sky, and then they'd appeared and she'd promptly collapsed into an induced cloud. In the last shred of her consciousness she scolded herself for what was, really, not at all appropriate behaviour for a spy.

Then there it was, plain as day, sounding in memory. Her father, his voice.

You were born and all the caterpillars everywhere sent out wishes for wings so they might flit and flop through limbs and dew and dripping green to land in your tiny palm.

She'd been seven years old when he'd sunk into the bed as though the mattress were swallowing him into some other world. But to his end, he smiled. He beamed at her as she made him tea, not too hot; as she walked from his bedside to the shore with such purpose, to dab at him with a washcloth made wet with salt; as she read from the newspaper, haltingly, with commentary, sharing her conclusions on global bombings and international market crashes and local cats that rang doorbells. He watched her, paying attention, and took one last lesson to task, for her.

When you run, girl, and your heart thumps in your chest, all the stars tug at their pins.

He had been a poet, a very small man who lived in a very small cabin in the middle of what was neither an island nor a spit. At low tide Missy would poke at crabs and collect smooth glass until the sea overcame the bridge of beach, sending her scampering back to their home before pebbles went underwater again. He had taught her to plant and light fire and build shelter and everything else that was worthy, the kind of math and art and science that would leave his girl in need of nobody. It had mostly been just the two of them, more companions than father and daughter. When he noticed that her hearing had begun to fail, he put his hands on her shoulders, sharp blue eyes level with hers. *Never mind, little fox,* he said to her firmly. *What's that you*

got there? Not one but two strong legs. Look at those muscles. All the
world was made for you.

He had loved her mother too, a big-rig driver filled with
wanderlust. She'd drive off across the country for weeks and
months at a time, sending them postcards along the way. Then
the postcards stopped coming, and so did she.

Mairi had seen a one-legged seagull lying crumpled under a
dock one day, looking peaceful, but it was dead. She knew what
that meant but she liked poetry too. Again and again she would
ask her father *What happened to mama?* and they would curl
up in front of the hearth that filled one wall of their wooden
home. Sparks popped and embers glowed and he spun the story,
framing her.

Your mama, one day she was swallowed up by a giant blue
whale and inside its belly she found an empire, and she became its
queen, and the whole ocean sparkles with diamonds for her, and she
commands the whale to take her wherever she wishes, and sits on a
throne of kelp silk, and icebergs and volcanoes bow to her through the
curtain of its baleen grin.

(In her sleep the girl smiled faintly, and the two pirates who
discussed her fate paused.)

By all your blood and your bone, I won't be just your father
anymore. I will be your go-go-go. I will see everything you see. You'll
feel my smile through the darkest black.

She remembered him fading, but never afraid. He was on his
way to find the whale and be its king. His daughter was only

seven, but she knew. To her this was a truth as sure as worms in spring.

Whenever you are sad all you need to do is look down. Under your feet you'll see dirt. Millions and millions of miles of dirt on this great big ball of earth, and you make it spin with every step you take. Never feel sorry for yourself. You have been loved! You have been loved enough for ten lives, for a hundred, for a thousand.

Little Mairi gave her father the only thing she could: obedience. She would heed him and never be afraid, never be sad for herself for being motherless and then fatherless.

One day, people came to take them both away. He to be looked after, an empty body, and she to be looked after, a fully alive girl. They hammered a FOR SALE sign into the earth in front of the little cabin. They brought her to another family, and then another, and another. Random houses, most of whom were dutiful but puzzled by her. *Such an odd girl.* She kept quiet mostly, appreciated small kindnesses, ran off now and then, and sometimes returned. She was chased by government people quite a bit. When they caught up with her they'd cluck at her disapprovingly. She didn't mind. She simply moved, and kept moving, and saw all she could see, knowing the spirit of him was inside her, fused with her thumping heart.

• • •

The pirate set down her cloth. The cot creaked as she settled herself beside the unexpected apprentice, who twitched in her sleep as though she dreamed of running.

"Do you ever stop, strange child?" Pip spoke softly, brushing Missy's matted hair from her forehead. "Do you?"

• • •

"*Oki*, Chief. Best to you." The captain reached out and clasped the older man's hand warmly.

"And to you, *Sipiapo*. It's good to have you back."

The arbour looked different in the daytime. It was surrounded by a village on its far side, streets lined with cabins and houses and a drive-in and a hockey rink and everything anyone could need within walking distance of the Griffons' soddie camp. Lou was there, the drummer. He winked at Missy across the gap between the two tribes, pirates and Bloods. Missy bowed her head, flushing as she remembered eagles and buffalo, feeling silly for expecting to see them that way on an ordinary Monday morning. Instead, they wore jeans and carried thermoses of coffee, as of course they would. Missy felt a tap on her arm. It was Birdie.

"We're goin' to Lou's. He's got a trampoline. Want to come?"

"Sure." The girls walked through the grasses and onto asphalt toward the town.

"Me and Cirrus are Bloods," said the metalsmith. They had turned a corner and picked through woods that spilled out into a backyard peppered with tricycles and soccer balls. Birdie unzipped the netting and they climbed through. The trampoline was warm, a pocket of heat, and they sat there a while, sprawling this way and that.

"Captain wrenched a company looking to divert our river. They stole caterpillar tracks from the diggers, laid metal netting in the ground around the banks, made it a hassle for the suits. And so the suits went away. That was when I was a kid. Now, there's more than ever to be done. Big Oil puttin' pipelines through, all of them bound to mess up the water and the air…"

"What do they call him, the captain?"

"*Sipiapo*. Night-walker. For when he works."

"Natives and pirates. Still can't decide if it makes perfect sense or none at all." Birdie turned at the sound of Lou's voice as he appeared from around the corner of the house. He approached the netting with his thermos in one hand and a squirming baby in the other, and paused for Missy's eye.

"Natives and your Newfoundlanders and people from all over work those oil sands. Plenty make money there and sometimes I think maybe it's not so bad as they say. We need oil and gas, right? But the way it's happenin'…got a friend in Fort Chipewyan who can light his kitchen tap on fire. Bottomless sick-and-poisoned, and bottomless gold. Guess which one wins." He joggled from one foot to the other. "You know how many barrels' worth of oil are buried in that dirt up north? 170 billion."

"170 billion…" Missy murmured.

"They figure this one's gonna clean it up." He squeezed his baby, a dimpled plump girl with tufts of jet-black hair.

"Paa paa ba baaa!" she said. It was time for a nap.

"...But there's forty-two thousand jobs, near ten thousand of 'em got by people like us. Everyone's gotta eat. Industry feeds 'em. What can you do?"

He sipped from his thermos, and his baby's eyes drooped, and Missy remembered the voice of Rasmus Krook, muttering as he did his rounds, giving her a first glimpse of the what and the why of the Griffons. *The people will pay with their whole being: physically, mentally, ideologically, spiritually, with their land, their soul. And not just country people. Not just Native people. Poison will flow through villages, towns, and cities and not stop. We must rise up. We must disrupt the system. Capitalism is a deception.*

"You can help pirates," she said, because that's the only answer she knew. Lou lifted his coffee in salute, and Missy stood up to jump.

Chapter Ten

FLICKA MISSING

FROM: International Union, Treasure Hunters &
Useful Goods Salvagers Society
Eastern Seaboard Headquarters, Halifax,
Nova Scotia

TO: The Bramble, Dread Crew Maritime Base
Guardians & Associates of Mairi MISSY Bullseye
(UNACCOMPANIED MINOR)

c/o Joe THE JACKAL Sponagle

RE: Overdue paperwork

Captain Gristle: As you are aware, the apprentice
in your care (herein referred to as "Missy") was
scheduled to return to the Dread Crew base two
weeks ago. Enclosed is the paperwork to complete
her transition from her most recent workterm with
the CRUMMIES of northern Hudson Bay to a special
union assignment. Your signature is required. This
paperwork is required in triplicate, delivered no
later than five (5) business days after the receipt
of this registered package. THANK YOU.

"What's that mean, two weeks ago?" Anneke leaned in across the table.

"Just like it says." Dan read it again, this time to himself, while Joe sat frowning and scratching absently at his beard. "She was supposed to be back by now. She is not. We knew she was late."

"You knew she was late?" Eric's mother, who felt responsible for Missy as they all did, sat back on the bench feeling confused to the point of delinquent.

"We did." Hector stepped into the light from the corner of the kitchen.

"So did I." Eric pulled her last postcard from the pocket of his hoodie and handed it to his mother.

"It's not unusual, especially for a young apprentice as useful as Missy. Crews would stall before returning an apprentice like her," Joe muttered. "Right, Hector?"

Hector did not respond.

Anneke softened. "All right, then. Where is she?"

"No way of knowing. I sign that paper, I'll be givin' my permission for somethin' they already done. She's away. That's 'bout as much as we'll ever know till she's not."

Wood crackled lightly in the stove, and the maple tea that simmered on the back burner bubbled a little. In the impasse, Eric rose wordlessly and went through the hall and up the back stairs.

"We've got to make for Maine, soon, Cap'n," said Vince. "If we don't do the loop through New England before snow flies, we'll miss the season down there."

"Enough," Hector growled.

Joe stood up from his place at the table. He brought his supper plate to the sink, chose an apple turnover from the stovetop, and poured himself a mug of tea. He then turned around, facing friends and collaborators. They watched him, as they always did in times like this. The old man took a bite of pastry and chewed thoughtfully.

"Delicious, Anneke." He wiped a smear of icing sugar from his chin with a dishcloth and walked through the kitchen with his tea, headed for the back stairs. "There's only one of us doin' the right thing right now, and that's our tracker."

By the time everyone made their way up the stairs and up the pull-down ladder to the attic, Eric had turned on the light and tugged on the roll-down schoolhouse map. It retracted with a clack-clack-clack, revealing a truer map underneath—also titled NORTH AMERICA but littered with pinpricks, colour-coded tags, and threaded paths. Hector, Vince, Sam, and Meena leaned toward it.

"You…" Hector traced a finger along a piece of green yarn that stretched from Nova Scotia to Maine. A tiny tag hung from one end of a pin rooted just inland from Bridgewater: *D.C.* A living map of piracy.

"I've been listening, that's all." Eric opened a roll-top desk that had always been in the shadow of the corner, revealing a small black box. Vince stiffened.

"That's eavesdroppin', kid."

"Not if you're a friend. If you're a friend it's just listening."

"The union closes those channels for a reason. You are not a pirate."

Joe stepped forward. "Vince, Missy went away and I think our Eric wanted to have a sense of what she's been up to, that's all. We all do."

"I'm a tracker. I can't help it." Eric shifted uncomfortably under the first mate's disapproval.

"The Bombs…" Hector turned to the map and moved west. "They's just a pin. They're not movin'. What's this timeframe? A month?"

"Bobcat one, bobcat two. That's code for Brunhilda and Fritzi. Their cave network is here, in the Black Tusk range." He touched a yellow pin, and looked at his parents and Joe to relay to them what the pirates, engrossed and whispering in front of the map, already knew.

"The Bombadiers go anywhere there's mountains. *Ulric* and *Ursidae* are their ships. They've got tracks for earth and blades for snow. Right now they've had to stop for some refit, here." He pointed to a red thumbtack deep in the Cariboos.

Vince turned from the map to the boy. He was without menace now, curious in the way one clever man admires the work of another. "How'd you get the codes?"

"Joe wrote to the chief. Said he may as well be able to listen so he'd know when to expect new crews for honey training.

They said yes. They figure he's no risk cause he's just—"

"—one old coot," Joe interrupted, lifting his steaming mug in salute.

Eric gestured south from the Dread Crew pin to a green thumbtack fixed upon New York City. "The Cleaners—that's what they call the Skels. They've got a fleet of junk trucks and pose as municipal workers. They're pulling down a warehouse tonight."

He pointed to the middle of the blue between Nova Scotia and Spain. "Every now and then they see Maddock Llewelyn in Halifax. The Meaner Submariners are at the Bottom for maintenance. They checked in last week but it's a weak signal. They're a long way underwater. Plus he's Welsh and his accent's so thick I can't catch much of it."

Meena chuckled, nodding. She'd met Llewelyn once. His mother looked confused.

"The Bottom is their base," he explained, pointing to another yellow tack. "It's a bathysphere, here."

"They don't hear much from Terra Juanita—she's captain of the Excavadoras. They're too far south to deal much with Halifax. They report to the headquarters in Argentina. The Cazas are busy too, but they're in the Mediterranean and we only get word of them if something goes wrong at the depot in Palermo."

Hector muttered, nodding at the map.

"There are too many other crews to keep track of. I hear a lot of names and places I don't know. More captains than I can count.

The union officials get on the B channel and share news of the faraway crews. They think nobody's listening except themselves."

Vince stepped around Meena, who was still engrossed in the Cariboos. "How's all this add up to what they've done with our Missy?"

Eric moved his hand over Ontario and Quebec. "Ripsaw Mick leads the Crummies. Abitibi Canyon is their base." A yellow tack in northern Ontario held two tags. One read *C*. The other read *M.B.* Ten days ago they were there, between jobs. Then they got called up to a place called Steep Rock."

His hand followed a piece of yarn stretching from Abitibi to northern Manitoba, to a single green thumbtack.

"She was with them when they left, and not with them when they got to the mine."

"How do you know?" Vince stopped pacing to stand in front of Eric.

"I heard someone from the Crummies calling in. Something about an apprentice transfer. It was on their way to Steep Rock, where they turned north from Winnipeg. Then later, I heard a union official on the closed channel. I think he was talking to the chief. I can't be sure."

The attic went silent.

"I've never heard them say anything like this before. Someone said, *Little B deployed for reconnaissance, code crook.*"

Hector reached for the bench and sat down. Vince sat down beside him.

"Captain, they'd never…she'd never. We's all crooks. Maybe she meant 'catch up' with the Bombs. Maybe she's gone farther west. Maybe…" Vince looked fruitlessly at the map.

"Not crooks. With-a-K. Krook. His name is Rasmus and he leads the Griffs." The room gasped at Hector's read of it. Joe nodded in agreement.

"We don't know why," he said. "We don't know how the union's involved. They might've coerced her. But that doesn't change that the Barrow has to make for New England. The last thing we need right now is the union on your backs because you're low on junk."

Hector nodded grimly and stood up, making for the stairs. The rest followed out the front door and into the yard to collect at the Barrow's stern. It was here that Joe spoke again.

"You'll be back in a few weeks and by then, we'll have some answers. Don't let on that you know. Stay in touch with the union like always. Get junk. Eric and I will figure out what's next, and we'll let you know if we hear anything."

After a silence, Hector nodded reluctantly. "We leave it in home hands for now."

Joe patted Eric's shoulder and went downstairs with Anneke and Dan. Johnny, Meena, Sam, Willie, and the rest of the crew interpreted the moment correctly as a ready-order, filing back down through the attic hatch and out to the yard, where they wordlessly reported to their stations, rolling up canvas tarps and stowing food and warming the engine, preparing to depart.

Home hands. Eric, left by himself in the attic, looked down at his own. They were smaller, it seemed, than those of a pirate.

•••

From the top of the ridge Eric could see all the way down the old Burne road, an unpaved stretch of backwoods transport that led eventually to the network of logging roads and obsolete highways that went across the province, up into New Brunswick, and then around and south. The great wooden Barrow had rolled away from the Bramble trailing a column of smoke behind it, then lurched over the crest of the hill, leaving everything in his field of vision just as it always had been. Trees undisturbed, jack pines thick like weeds. Neighbours taking a stroll after supper, enjoying the scent of warm soil, hopes high for a gentle fall. Even the animals stretched out languorously, enjoying the sweetness in the air. But Eric Stewart was not content.

He walked miserably along the ridge, feeling left behind. He stared at his boots shuffling through the grass, thinking of his first discovery—that cracked Barrow hubcap—and then clues, everywhere. Then the pirate invasion. Then she'd shown up in his attic, rifling through his things.

CRACK. Joe's axe rang out from beyond the ridge. *When I can't see straight with worry,* he'd said once, *I split wood. Makes my shoulders ache for days, but at least then I'm worryin' about what's left of my muscles instead of whatever I was worryin' about.*

CRACK. CRACK. CRACK.

•••

"Whoop Up, this is Stand Off."

"Hey, Lou. How you been?"

"Waitin' on parts all day long, so the shop's backed up bad. See anything up there tonight?"

A hundred kilometres away, Councilman Jimmy First Runner shifted the phone and closed one door then another behind him until he stood alone in his workshop, his family's supper muffled and distant.

"The oil company made another quarter-mile today, down as far as Fish Creek," he whispered. "*Sipiapo* was right. Our friends lifted those chunks outta the line off the new end but that only made them triple security. I've sent Will out with the truck. He's gonna check the north section and tell us what he sees."

Lou nodded. "Any cameras?"

"None so far. But they got a consultant down from Beaver Hills, so who knows. Some ex-cop. Soon, maybe. But tonight I'd say they're not watching the middle. Got a call from May up in Red Deer and she's sayin' it's been light up there. Will's gonna give the all-clear. He's got a moth with him. He'll let 'em know."

Later that night Lou sat, brow furrowed, on his front porch. A bunch of high school kids walked by on their way to the main drag. A tall, saggy figure on a BMX bike caught Lou's eye as he passed. It was Nadine's boy. He raised a fist in the air.

"Fight the power! *Kainai!*" he yelled, standing on his pedals. Two girls giggled and the others snickered and shoved each other, tumbling on down the street.

Yeah, he thought. *You don't know half of it, kid.*

• • •

Rolf was assigned with orienting the girl, and Missy followed him outside for her first proper ship walkabout. The steel-woolishness of him was familiar to her. Smudgy eyes, a Gristle beard, a heavy gait. *Like he's carrying something nobody else can see.* He knocked on the hull and she snapped to attention.

"Helicopters are the least efficient flying machine. They're hunks of metal that would rather stay on the ground," he said. "Without wings, they don't have much natural glide. We've got to fight to get them afloat and keep them that way."

Missy looked up. "But this isn't a helicopter."

"That's right." They walked a perimeter, the Avenger sitting on her haunches. "She is a tilt rotor aircraft. She's got four prop rotors."

"They rotate, right?" Missy pointed to the shafts at the end of the ship's fixed wings.

Rolf studied her curiously. "You know aircraft?"

Missy shrugged. "Not really."

"We land like a helicopter," He mimicked a descent with his hands. *Give her the basics*, Rasmus had said. *Just enough.* "We get into tight spots. We don't need landing strips. With rotors, all we need is a clear patch of grass and down we go."

"You land like a helicopter and…"

He looked encouragingly at her, nodding at the wings.

"You fly like a plane. The rotors tilt and turn into propellers."

"For speed. Risk is vigor. Vigor is life. Just like the good captain said, girl."

There was a shrewdness in his eyes. Missy turned to take in the staging ground of open land, the crew having spilled out to a broader spread of stations. A fresh plume of smoke rose from the soddie longhouse, Pip at the task of the night's meal. Taro, up high, scrambled from one rotor to the next with his toolbox. Cirrus, with the help of Billy, had dismantled a section of hydraulics for servicing, engine guts and bones laid out atop a folding table in the open air. Birdie worked inches from the hull, her face shielded, mending imperfections with spark and flame on a patch of metal stencilled FUEL INTAKE.

"I have a lot of questions."

And I have to report back on your answers, but you don't know that. Rolf smiled behind his beard. "Pick one."

"You've defected from the union. You're a plane and a helicopter. Both those things need a lot of money and parts and..." She gestured at the stencil. "Fuel. How can you just disappear—run away—and keep flying? Who pays for it? Why? Are you still pirates? Where's your junk?"

The coxswain smiled again. "Like I said. Pick one."

Missy thought for a moment. "Why are you up here?"

"We have a job to do. There's a pipeline goin' in. We're trying to stop it."

"No, I mean you. Why are *you* up here?"

His face darkened. "Penance. Next question."

Chapter Eleven

CONGREGATION

The beacon at Cree Lake, Saskatchewan, rose like a flagpole from the roof of an abandoned hunting lodge, a longhouse just as woodsy as a soddie was grassy. Missy felt higher up on the map in this northernmost outreach of boreal woods where the fish were fat and the bears were too. It was foreign again, different from the tangled cragginess of the east and the sea-like waves of the long plains. One day, one flight, and everything had changed.

"…Free fatty acids, that's triglycerides. Then decarboxylation. That leaves you with alkanes, or straight-chain hydrocarbons of either 15 or 17 carbon atoms. That's the starting point for whatever kind of fuel we want to make. From there, we change the recipe to suit. We reset the turbines for ethanol long ago. Turboboosters for thin air, an EPU generator, additives to keep the engine from freezing or exploding. Make sense?"

Missy's furrowed brow made Gwynne smile.

"Let me say it simply. We start with raw fat—onion ring grease!—and turn it into fuel. We're self-sufficient. We don't need the supply depots anymore. All that *and* we burn clean.

Onion rings don't make soot."

Missy sat on a bench, her head spinning as the pirates launched into a debate on the finer points of compression ignition. She squinted, trying her best to follow the volleys of group discussion. As ever, she managed by patching bits together. Defection, then freedom. An angry union. Fuel sources from Thunder Bay to Yellowknife to Kamloops stalked by a bird of prey: hamburger restaurants, industrial cafeterias, commercial food factories. Even untended chip trucks, for all the spectacle of pausing to pick it dry. All that could be found in the morning were forced locks and emptied vats, for these pirates were nocturnal and light of foot, and craved altitude like sustenance, and that is all anyone knew, at least from the ground.

Gwynne sat with her chair tipped back. "…Combustion and viscosity at the same time—that's always been the trick. Nobody could do it."

"Until you," Missy interjected, thinking aloud, as the significance of it all settled upon her.

"Right you are, *flicka!*" Rasmus bounded as he did into every conversation, appearing with a rush of wind through the longhouse door. He saluted through the window to the clearing where the ship rested. "We feed that thirsty beast and we do it all on our own."

"I get the how." Missy turned to face the captain. "You didn't need the union anymore. You made it so you'd not need anybody. But I don't get the why."

Missy looked around the table from one figure to the next. Taro, the bladesmith, with his hands in his pockets, casted his eyes low except for a tuft of raised eyebrow. Finola put down her mug and looked amused. Missy filled in the blank.

"Because…there are people who do bad things to rivers and wild land?"

One of the brutes chuckled. Another elbowed him. "Leave 'er be, Ginsberg. It's one thing to see a few headlines. She jus' meant to get a handle on the real view, eh?"

Two-Hands shrugged and Missy began again.

"I know there's such a thing as things done well. You can take certain trees that grow fast. But you shouldn't take them all. And you shouldn't take the old growth. And you shouldn't replant them all the same or they'll get wiped out by some beetle. And you shouldn't take them with machines that crush everything else."

She looked at the faces, all of them suddenly quieted at this answer that went well beyond correct. She took a sip and said the only remaining thing. "My dad liked trees."

Rasmus smiled behind his mug. Then everyone turned to Rolf, who leaned against the hull chewing on an unlit pipe. He had said something. Once he had the floor as well as Missy's eye, he spoke directly to her across the crowd.

"I took the trees and scraped the whole of the forest floor bare. Made a wasteland all scarred up with craters, drivin' our bulldozers without care beyond speed and money. We'd leave twenty or thirty trees in a clump. We'd show that to the inspector, just enough to not get stamped as clear-cutters. One good storm and that last patch would topple. Years of it and pockets of cash, but Clayoquot Sound finished me."

The air became very thick and still.

"Clayoquot Sound…" said Missy softly.

He looked darkly at her. "Ever seen a two-thousand-year-old tree, girl?"

Missy shook her head. Many others nodded slowly.

"A two-thousand-year-old tree watches you. I walked into a grove of them and I had my orders, and if it wasn't me it would be the next guy, so I started cutting. Ancient wood smells different when it bleeds. But I kept going until it was done. I couldn't even look up for all them watching me. I didn't just cut down trees. I made two thousand years extinct, with my saw, over and over again. I felt like a murderer. Wish I'd felt that way sooner, for them and for every measly little twenty-year pine. But I didn't. Not till Clayoquot. I made a living of turning gods into…junk."

That's the heavy thing he carries, she thought. Rolf nodded as though he'd heard inside her head.

The captain stood up next to him. "You were one of them. But then you looked up."

He lifted a fist, where it hung, waiting. Rolf clenched his hand and they pressed knuckles, a mutual nod. Missy felt, at that moment, like she'd only just looked up.

"Bannock, comrades." Pip pushed through the huddle
in front of the fire with a steaming tray. There was a rush
of grateful arms and hands. For a while it was all sighs and
contented chewing, and sparks from good, dry wood, and the
pleasant rarity, for the pirates, of footing that was grounded
and still. Rasmus approached the bench, dragging a small stool
across the floorboards. He sat across from Missy, level to her
face, and met her eyes.

"The why, Bullseye, is this. We are the only ones with a single
view of how one sort of destruction bleeds into another."

High in the sky, the remote lands of the midwest had clicked
like puzzle pieces into a picture vast and ominous. Like the
trans-northern pipeline, always growing. *That evil snake*, Rasmus
called it, his nemesis that slithered hungrily across the land.
That plus unscrupulous logging and mining, diverted waterways,
unchecked industrial waste—all of it had a cumulative effect on
forests, human health, and wildlife patterns, each zone watched
by disconnected government departments and activist groups,
none of them able to fully grasp it all. Not like airborne pirates.

With a nudge to her left shoulder, Cirrus passed a warm tin
bowl to Missy. She took another hunk with a nod and passed it
on to Magnus, who sat on her right. Baked over hot coals, the
biscuit-bread was crispy and fluffy with bursts of seedy tartness.
It's a forsaken mess but it all goes down fine as gold, Pip had said
earlier that afternoon as she picked industriously through one
of many camp galleys. *Flour, butter, salt, fire. Don't take much.*

Missy dipped the bannock into her mug and sighed contentedly. Magnus was speaking now.

"…But they've gone and diverted rivers for the loggers, and they do it for irrigation, and mining. Water gets pushed to serve industry and then it flows back into the river system too warm, deoxygenated, full of pesticides and chemicals. Poison that no living thing can tolerate. Then cars spew carbon monoxide. Factories spew sulfur dioxide. Power plants spew nitrogen oxides…"

Rasmus interjected. "Spew! All of it spew, *flicka lilla*. It's coal and petroleum and everything that stunts growing things. It makes asthma and cancer and acid rain. It gets into water and soil and air and chokes cities with smog."

"In August, we can fly barely a thousand feet over Bloor Street and nobody sees a thing," added Ginsberg, his mouth full of biscuit, his face a mix of boastfulness and disbelief. "They're all just down there runnin' for the bus."

Rasmus was pacing now, talking with his hands. "Sustainable harvesting of renewable resources, that's what they call it. Shakespeare said, 'Pardon me, thou bleeding piece of earth, that I am meek and gentle with these butchers.' This is no harvest. This is a ghastly pillage. And we ought not to be meek and gentle in our witnessing of it."

"Can you stop it?" Missy interjected, and the captain stopped pacing to turn to her. "Can anybody?"

"No," he said simply. "We delay, stall, count small victories.

But they always come back with more money, more machines, more pipe."

Magnus stepped forward. "We have a chance with the trans-northern, Captain." His first mate wanted to convince his captain as much as himself. "We've cut it seventeen times. Eighteen as of next week. We'll make it so they can never switch it on. As quick as they finish repairing one stretch, we'll chop another."

"The oil will flow as long as human beings stay lazy and thirsty…" Rasmus descended into madness or ascended into brilliance depending on where you stood—for rage and vitality, crime and justice, and terrorist and activist were the prickles and fruit of one same bramble. Missy's eyes began to droop and she drifted.

Rope in her hands, coarse and prickly as she climbed it. The apple tree she'd jumped from in the pouring rain, scrambling through the gutter and across the Barrow's topdeck. From there to a blacklist and a deal cut with the boss of all captains and a wounded earth and dancing eagles and a boy standing in a blackberry orchard and here is where it all finally made sense— over moss tea and bannock during the gospel of Rasmus Krook.

She's not listening, thought Rolf. *Not anymore, not even in her way. She remembers something else.*

• • •

YOU CUT CORNERS? WE CUT PROFITS. ~ G
DO WRONG, GET WRONGED. ~ G

Missy leaned over the boy's shoulder as he lettered black ink on white canvas, a material sturdy enough to exist among the flotsam of environmental warriorship. To be received by those who had earned them, the Griffons' calling cards had to endure weather, wind, and destruction.

"Most people who monkeywrench mean well, but they're artless thugs. That's what Dad calls them."

"Your dad's a monkeywrencher too? Does he know you're a pirate?" Missy was entranced.

"He was an activist," the boy replied, cutting more canvas and stacking it neatly. "He got put in jail a lot with Rasmus back in the day. They're both Swedish. Ras used to hang out at our house before he was a pirate. They did a lot of planning at our kitchen table. My dad mellowed out. He's a biologist now. Does what he can, releases studies and stuff. Not Rasmus, though. He stayed mad and disappeared. Dad figures he's off in the bush, jackbootin' trees. Pretty much true. My dad thinks I'm at a boarding school for gifted kids. That's pretty much true too."

They both smiled.

"Anyways. People try to blow up pipelines and end up making a spill. Or they spike trees and hurt loggers when the real bad guys are the ones who wear the suits."

RETRIBUTION. ~ G

Jesper finished with the stylized "G" and set the note aside to dry.

"What makes a good monkeywrench?" Missy rested her chin in her hands, looking at him with interest.

He reached to the shelf behind him to retrieve a large book bound in linen, brown and well-used. A row of books just like it sat in a neat row, each of them categorized and dated. He placed it on the table in front of her and opened it randomly, a vast sheet of grid paper filled with lettering so meticulous it looked like architectural drawings.

Missy scanned the page, shaking off how his trust made her feel. "What's all this for?"

"Without records, scientists have nothing but theories," he replied.

"Is that what the captain says?"

"No. That's what I say. See? Look here. Artful."

Missy followed to where he pointed, running her own finger along the grid to piece together one story of dozens. "To protest a proposed strip mine in northern Manitoba—in Leaf Rapids, it says here—the crew spent a year pulling up surveyors' stakes. Really? That's it?"

"Yeah," he said. "The company couldn't dig a single hole. They kept sending in people to mark out where the mine would be. They'd set stakes in the day. We'd take them out at night. Eventually, the corporation lost its license."

"And that was that?" Missy was rapt.

He nodded. "For a few years. Lots of it is pretty simple. We munch logging roads with nails. We grind down sawblades so they can't cut, chop down the power lines to factory slaughterhouses. We cap smokestacks. Let 'em get a lungful of their own burp…"

Missy turned again to the record book. Neat script had been added next to an entry about adding horse manure and marbles to the water intake of a paper mill.

Modern technology has a low tolerance for old-fashioned protest.
~ RK

She looked up at him. "You guys are still pirates, you know. It's all right here."

The pirate boy opened his mouth to speak but then looked up at the intercom.

(CLEARED FOR TAKEOFF, BEACON TWO-NINER. WESTWARD TWO-SEVEN-ZERO TO BEACON ONE-FOUR.)

The ship lurched as it left the ground, Missy sensing the static, vibration, and velocity of the Avenger's rise into the sky.

Chapter Twelve

COURSE OF ACTION

"*It's* waterproof."

Birdie took the sheet of paper, filmy-thin, and rolled it tight. Then she slipped it into the tube and closed the cap, and held the message moth up to the light between her thumb and forefinger. After fastening the note to its underbelly, she set it legs-down on the table and plugged it into a laptop computer.

"We program the destination—" She typed the address into the computer. "Then off it goes. It stays pretty high until it's over the target, then it dives."

It was a pretty thing, a silvery dark grey with transparent wings stretched over a metal skeleton and antennae to confirm delivery. It was eerily true to life except for its lack of eyes and mouth—a wordless, sightless creature—and its giant size, making it a pirate in the realm of everyday moths.

"Does it come back?"

"Depends on how far," she said. "We talk to friends this way. Mostly, they just save them for us to use again."

"What if it's got a long way to go?" It seemed too delicate for such a big sky. "I mean, my note…"

"That's one of the best parts." Birdie reached behind her and turned back around with a small metal circle in the palm of her hand. "Gwynne came up with a long-life battery. It can't cross the sea. Not yet. But it can go from one side of the country to the other, or almost. It may take a few days, but it's faster than Canada Post. It can sure make it to…where, again?"

Missy rose from the table with the moth in her hand.

"Nova Scotia. The Bramble, to…" She halted. "To the Dreads."

Dear Eric. August 14.

I found the Griffons. I'm with them. They're on the run but now I know why. It's a good reason. I'll tell you later. You can't write to me. Only me to you. Sorry about that.

Missy

P.S. I'll miss getting post cards from you with all the news.

P.P.S. Don't worry about sending the moth back. Hang on to it for me.

P.P.P.S. If the chief calls don't tell her I'm here.

FLYGPOST

Cirrus, passing with his toolbox, stopped beside her and looked from her face to the moth and back again. He reached out and grasped the handle of the stern porthole.

"We're low enough," he said, giving the handle a twist and a pull. With a whoosh it opened to the sky, a slot just wide enough to accommodate the moth in flight. He gestured to it and patted her on the shoulder.

"Thanks," said Missy. The pirate gave a little bow, smiled, and walked away. Missy turned the switch and the moth hummed in her hand. She perched it on the porthole ledge, and could have sworn that it stretched its wings. Then with a flutter it was gone.

• • •

"Mom. I'm fourteen. I know how to get a cab."

"But you've never been anywhere. What if there's a problem with the plane and you get stuck? What if you go to the wrong gate?"

(It was going to happen, Eric knew it, or his mother wouldn't be so unlike herself.)

It was a delicate and unprecedented moment at the new Dread Crew homebase—The Bramble, as the pirates had named the Stewart family's rambling old farmhouse and wild woods. Dan put his hand on his wife's shoulder and pulled her aside to whisper in her ear. "Cecil's daughter called back. She'll get us a discount, and you've got your points. It won't cost much, and she said she'll sign up to work his flight and she'll keep an eye out for him."

Practical barriers fell away, leaving not more than a vague uncertainty.

"I can follow directions, Mom. I'll be okay."

His mother looked from her son to her husband and back again. "Linnea doesn't have a car, but she'll be expecting you. You've got her address. We'll tell her everything. You can stay with her overnight until your flight back home."

Eric nodded. He hadn't seen his aunt—his mother's sister—in a couple of years, but he was glad to have her on the other end of all this.

"Everyone, sit. Let's run through this one more time." Joe ushered Eric and his parents to the kitchen table. "Anneke, more tea?"

She nodded and he refilled her mug, passing it to her. He pulled a chair to the table.

"Missy is some kind of pawn. We haven't heard from her in some time, but we know that the union is using her, somehow, to find the Griffons. We also know that the Griffons don't want to be found."

Eric nodded. Joe continued.

"Then there's what we don't know. We don't know if she knows she's a pawn. We don't know what Rasmus Krook will do when he finds out she's led the union to them. We don't know why the Griffons don't want to be found. We don't know what they're doing up there, if it's against the law or dangerous or something that's going to put Missy in harm's way. We need more information. So. Eric—"

The boy, flanked by his mother and father, leaned forward.

"You'll go to the union depot in Winnipeg. Your name is John Green."

Again, a nod.

"You work in the metals division of the municipal recycling plant. You are reporting to the depot because someone's offered you a bribe to divert scrap to the union. You're there to meet with the deputy manager."

"What if they don't let me in? What if they don't believe me? What if—"

"Eric, tell me again exactly what time you will show up."

Eric exhaled in a whoosh. *Joe knows what he's doing.* "Five past noon."

"Exactly," Joe clapped once. "The deputy manager is a bureaucrat, so he'll be in line for a double-double and an apple cruller. The administrative office will be empty, other than the receptionist, who'll send you—John Green—in to wait."

"And then?" Eric asked. Joe sat back, both hands in the air.

"...I look for records. Or reports. Or a file on the Griffons. It's their region. Maybe if there's a computer I'll be able to find out where she is."

"And then?" Anneke looked at her son.

"Then I get out. And we get Missy back home."

•••

To Chief August 17.
Sorry it took me a little longer but I found them. I am on the ship. I don't know yet where they'er going or why. But I'm here and I'm watching, like you said to.
Missy

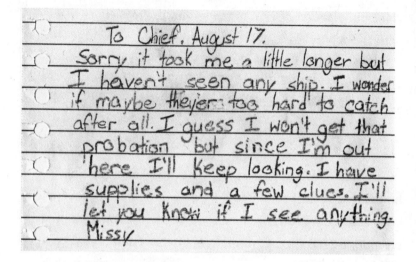

To Chief. August 17.
Sorry it took me a little longer but I haven't seen any ship. I wonder if maybe they'er too hard to catch after all. I guess I won't get that probation but since I'm out here I'll keep looking. I have supplies and a few clues. I'll let you know if I see anything.
Missy

One note would fulfill her duty. The other would be a lie. Missy looked at them laid side by side on her cot. After some time she lifted one, folded it neatly, and slipped it into the envelope. She licked it shut, stamping it with Bobby Orr, HOCKEY LEGEND OF PARRY SOUND. The other she slipped into the front pocket of her pack, rejected, because like it or not, it was the right thing to do.

("Ten degrees to starboard, Captain. Banking steady. Beacon two in sight. Just outside Fort McMurray."

"Excellent, Magnus, *tack. Ner på marken*. To the ground we go.")

Missy heard none of the order but felt it, the ship responding, gravity adjusting to the growl of descent. To resupply, to rest, and to post.

• • •

"It's a safe line, closed channel, union can't hear it, over—"

The radio crackled with static. The captain on the other end of the line hesitated, then pressed the button. "How's the eastern weather in Bluenose country, over?"

Joe smiled. "No avalanches in sight, Captain Faust, over."

"Yeah, we been stuck here since the spring's snowpack got soft. We're usin' the downtime for refurbishin'. How can I help you, Jackal, over?"

Fritzi Faust had heard of this Jackal Joe, friend of pirates. Word of the Dreads' change in tactics had travelled far, even to the highest and most remote peaks of British Columbia, and with it Joe's identity.

"I'm hoping you might have some information for me, over."

"I can tell ya what twelve metres of snow looks like."

"I bet you can. See, Fritzi—may I call you that?"

"You're a civilian. You can call me whatever you want."

"I'd like to know about some neighbours of yours, regionally speaking. I'd like to know about the Griffons, over."

There was a sudden emptiness in the air between the two radios. Then the call button went red and held red, the pirate captain on the other end considering, very carefully, her response.

"We don't speak of 'em much these days, over."

Joe let the emptiness stand, saying nothing in return and banking on Captain Faust to fill it. She did. After a long pause, the light went red again.

"The Griffs, Joe Jackal—I'll say it plain. That Rasmus Krook's a nutter." The line cracked out and then in again. "He thinks the bears and the trees should take over all the cities. He's on the national watchlist as a terrorist—that's federal prison—an' the union'll wash their hands of him soon as he's caught. I heard he's got every mining company an' logging company an' factory company west of Ontario after him, on both sides of the border, and the union on top of that. He's got a nerve that's ten feet tall an' reckless as they come. Why you wanna know, over?"

Joe listened, his head in his hands. *Oh Missy, girl.* His thumb hovered over the button before pressing it.

"Just going over my list of crews for consults. Union wouldn't tell me anything about these guys so I thought I'd ask. Curious, that's all, over."

"Curious is all anyone is," she replied. "Some say they've heard from 'em here and there. Pirates feel all kinds o' ways— some sympathetic, some not. If you need the union on yer side, though, you'd best never speak of 'em again. At best they're gone and at worst they've been snatched by the law and everyone with 'em, too, over."

Joe, already sunken with worry, sunk further.

"Fritzi, thanks. Appreciate it. Good luck with that snowpack, over."

The light went red again.

"Ten-four. Later, Jackal." Then silence, just black.

Chapter Thirteen

THE JOURNEY OF JOHN GREEN

This wasn't the first time Eric had done something big on his own, especially in the past year or two. He'd piloted a pirate ship. He had been put in charge of the bramble and kept the books as the junk poured in. But this was the first time he hadn't just stumbled into a big thing by accident. This time, it felt like an assignment. His mother had argued to come with him at first, and he'd made an impassioned speech at supper. *I'm old enough,* he'd said. *My friends have jobs. It's almost that time for me, and I've done more than all of them put together.* His mother's face changed from resistance to a proud sort of resignation. His father had already known: With his parents occupied with the market season, and with Joe required to man the home radio, this task was Eric's.

Through the truck window, he scanned the sky for planes. A sign on the off-ramp said CANADA'S OCEAN PLAYGROUND. COME AGAIN SOON. He wondered if there would be peanuts. The control tower came into view and a plane rose above it, taking off. Another turned toward the expanse of runway and Eric leaned toward it, as he did toward most things.

Later, after his parents and Joe had taken him as far as they could, and after hugs and more hugs, he walked down the gate hallway toward the open door, his backpack on his shoulder. There was a steady whoosh of forced air and pilots sitting in the cockpit with clipboards and weather reports. He tried to remember it all. *My name is John Green.* A flight attendant stood there smiling. *I work in the municipal recycling plant, in the metals division.* She reached out for his boarding pass and he gave it to her, and she waved him through, and he stepped into a giant metal tube with wings. *I'm selling inside information to divert metal scrap.* Seat 23E. He lowered himself into it and pushed his pack under the seat in front of him. *I'm here to meet with the deputy manager. He's expecting me.*

When the takeoff pressed him into his seat he thought his heart would jump out of his chest. Not because he was afraid, but because he was inside of something so improbable. *How can this thing fly?* But it did. He stared out the window at towns perched along the Trans-Canada, at river-threads that criss-crossed the land, at fields and posh houses with pools and unbroken swaths of trees, all of it rolled out in miniature like a play rug for dinkies.

You have your wallet? That money I gave you. Do you have it? Don't lose it. And don't check your bag. Your aunt will pick you up in arrivals. And call us. Call us, Eric, right away, as soon as you land. He knew what to do, but maybe his mom just needed to say it for herself. Maybe that was part of having a kid. Maybe you can't help but make sure they know what they need to know, even if you know they already know it.

It got darker and darker, and he saw stars and the moon like a spotlight, and he laid his head back, and then he woke up with a jolt and a crink in his neck. He had landed. He felt for his wallet. It was still there.

• • •

Linnea Betlam glanced at her watch. 11:32 AM. She took one last look at her nephew, who had grown unspeakably tall since she'd seen him last. He wore creased polyester pants and a crisp white shirt with a forged municipal ID badge pinned to his chest pocket. She fussed, pushing his cowlick down again with a wet hand.

"It's time," she said. The boy followed her down the stairs, his steps measured, to where she propped the front door open.

"The briefcase…"

"Here." She thrust the brown leather case into his arms. He stood in the doorway, fidgeting. He was taller now than her sister would be. She was sure of it.

"Thanks, Aunt Linnea. I'll be back for supper…I think."

"Yes. You will." A taxi pulled up in front of the house. He hugged her quickly and lingered on the front lawn. She gave him a thumbs-up and he crossed the sidewalk, opening the door and climbing into the back seat, the very picture of a young professional. *Perhaps too young?*

"Don't fidget!" she called after the cab as it disappeared down the street.

I don't know much about pirates, or about government people. But I'd bet none of them fidget.

Linnea returned inside and walked through her kitchen bound for the telephone. She would make a long-distance call, reporting, and then set two plates.

•••

The cab driver asked him three times if he was sure of the address. "There's nothin' out this way, kid. There hasn't been for twenty years."

Eric handed him a twenty-dollar bill. The car weaved around potholes through an abandoned industrial park and stopped in front of a boarded-up bowling alley with chains on the doors. Through peeling paint he read FRAMPTON'S FAIRLANES. The "L" hung upside-down. Knee-high grass swayed in the breeze through cracks in the concrete, and plywood concealed every window.

"This is it?" he said to the driver. "131 North Bend Road?"

"Yup. Like I said."

After the taxi had driven away, Eric stood there a while, his suit jacket bunching uncomfortably. He stepped forward and saw nothing you wouldn't expect to see on the front of a boarded-up bowling alley—except for the small security box with the button on the front. He pressed it haltingly. A voice answered.

"Yes?"

He moved closer.

"My name is J-John Green? I work in the municipal recycling plant, in the metals division. I'm here to speak about diverting some—"

BZZZZZZT. The door unlocked, sprung from inside. The chains, he could see now, were a false front. He heard a whirr and looked up to see the lens of a security camera, tucked into a corner behind a Pepsi sign, trained on him. Eric raised one hand, clutching his aunt's old briefcase with the other. *Makes you look like a manager*, she had said. He walked through the open door.

In the gloom of the alley, a wall of old shoe cubbies filled the wall behind a canteen advertising hot dogs for 75 cents. He took a confused step forward, scanning the cavernous room for signs of life. There was a dim light at the end of lane 8, the only thing to be seen. Above it was a bright white sign with a black arrow. *Down the... through the... they can't mean...*

"Proceed to lane 8, Mr. Green," said the voice from the security intercom.

He walked tentatively down the bowling lane, minding the gutters, his shoes hitting the wood with a clop-clop-clop. As he got closer, his eyes adjusted. Where the pins would have been, there was a door with a familiar insignia: a raised fist. He ducked under the pin guard. After another metal box, another button, and another camera, he was buzzed through into a series of hallways, each increasingly brighter and more tidy, the building connected to others in a way that was indiscernible from the front. Then he reached a waiting room. A receptionist looked up and waved him to a door with a plaque that read OFFICE OF THE DEPUTY MANAGER, CENTRAL/ WEST REGION.

"Go on in, but he's out on…business. You may have to wait a while."

He gestured a silent thanks, his heart pounding, and entered the office, taking a seat in the chair opposite the desk. It was plain and fantastic all at once. Filing cabinets, a fax machine, a computer left humming. One small window with wire netting strung across it. A folder marked DAILY ADVISORY REPORTS sat in a basket on the desk. With one last glance at the mostly-closed door to the waiting room (the receptionist was engrossed in her lunch), Eric rested his briefcase on the floor and flipped the cover of the folder open.

```
FROM: CHIEF, EASTERN HEADQUARTERS
TO: REGIONAL MANAGER, CENTRAL-WEST DIVISION
RE: NEW COPPER SCRAP GUIDELINES
```

Nope. He flipped to the next report.

```
FROM: CHIEF, EASTERN HEADQUARTERS
TO: REGIONAL MANAGER, CENTRAL-WEST DIVISION
RE: ON-SHIP LIVE ANIMAL PROTOCOL—UPDATE
```

Those Skels and their pet cobra…. A few more maintenance orders, two disciplinary actions, and then he stopped, gripping the edge of the desk.

FROM: CHIEF, EASTERN HEADQUARTERS

TO: REGIONAL MANAGER, CENTRAL-WEST DIVISION

RE: RECONNAISSANCE ADVISORY

MEMO: Young apprentice en route to aid in the
apprehension of blacklisted crew #18 code name:
BULLSEYE.

Female est. 13 years of age known as "Missy"
dispatched to intercept blacklisted crew. Exact time
of arrival to anticipated landing site unknown.
Awaiting confirmation by radio or union mail, or for
confirmed signal from GPS homing device among her
belongings. Central-west region is advised to be
diligent. If the girl is encountered, do not hinder
her. She is on special assignment and must believe
she is endorsed.

Further reports to follow.

END

With shaking hands he flipped the page.

FROM: CHIEF, EASTERN HEADQUARTERS

TO: REGIONAL MANAGER, CENTRAL-WEST DIVISION

MEMO:

BE ADVISED. GPS signal affirmative from apprentice
BULLSEYE. Device appears operational after battery
replacement and connector refit. Tracking will
commence if and when signal gains sufficient speed

and distance to be assumed airborne. Union response will initiate as soon as signal stabilizes for a minimum 48 hours, indicating a grounded period long enough to attempt recovery and arrest. Further reports to follow. Have begun campaign to inform local police.

END

The clock on the wall made an audible click as it moved to 12:28. Eric flinched, knocking the folder, and its contents fluttered to the floor. He swore under his breath and sank to his knees, scrambling, grabbing sheets and springing up again to put them back.

The door opened and the receptionist bent her head inside. "The deputy…oh! There you are. You're—what—"

He was on the wrong side of the desk. The deputy manager's side.

"Sorry, the wind blew some papers." Eric pointed at the window. It was closed. *Crap.* "I…shut it. Because of the wind. Then I picked them up. It's all here. They're all here."

He stumbled around to the visitor's side. "The deputy…?"

"The deputy is on his way. He was delayed in traffic."

Eric opted for his only way out: through. "Yes. About that. I'll have to reschedule."

"Reschedule?"

"Yes." He smiled solicitously as he pressed through the

doorway, sidling past her. "My bosses at the recycling plant expect me back. Can't let them get suspicious, can I? If they find out I'm diverting to a competing outfit…"

"A competing outfit…?"

"Please tell the deputy manager I'll be in touch. Goodbye."

"Goodbye?"

Puzzled, she stepped into the room and approached the window. Outside, nothing stirred. She turned and saw the young man's briefcase leaning against the chair.

"Mr.—come back!"

In her hands it felt unusually light. One clasp was broken. On a whim she flipped the other one and the case sprang open. With the exception of a pack of gum, a city bus transfer with a skull and crossbones doodled onto it, and a cellphone charger, it was empty.

Chapter Fourteen

ON THE THROTTLE

The postcard, slipped into Rolf's kit, said GREETINGS
FROM DAWSON CITY, YUKON: HEART OF THE
KLONDIKE. On the front was a row of can-can dancers. He
flipped it over. On the back was a juvenile scrawl.

Dear Rolf   August 21
I'm sorry about the old tree.
I didn't know how to say it so I sent
a postcard because my dad always
said everyone likes a postcard. I
don't think the trees are mad at
you anymore

Missy

(Rolf's Locker)

_____

_____

_____

•••

"Take these." Finola thrust a pair of headphones toward her.
"Standard for cockpit duty."

Missy looked, perplexed, at the equipment in her hands.

Finola was speaking with some degree of force, and she felt a strange breeze and vibration in the pit. *It must be loud up here.*

"These won't work for me." She looked questioningly at the pilot.

"They will for me," Finola replied. "I won't hear you unless you use the microphone. Continue to watch my speaking, that's fine. But you must talk to me through here."

She waggled the microphone that dangled off her own headphone, a mouthpiece. Missy nodded in response, lifting the apparatus over her head. The insulated rubber snapped tight to her head and she gave Finola a thumbs-up, taking her place in the cool, taut, black leather of the co-pilot's seat.

"Now, Missy. We fly." Finola gestured to the whole of the control panel. "How is that so? What do you see?"

From the first moment the wheels of the Avenger had lifted off the ground, Missy had been swept into a school of immersion. There was a context of crimes, punishments, and interventions to study. She cleaned the filters on the grease spigots, sorted charts, and saw more than half the beacons in the country as Rasmus and the crew flew a continual, watchful grid of the sky. But she had not, until now, been granted access to the cockpit. It was all spread out in front of her—a helm within reach—an array that shone and blinked like the inside of a treasure chest. She saw flashing lights and square knobs, sliders of all shapes and sizes. Readouts and computer screens projected flight patterns, destinations, wind direction. Some were encased behind Plexiglas, some with locks and switches. And in her silent world it was dizzying enough without the added dimensions of beeps and alarms, which were constant.

"I see it looks complicated."

"Oh, all this?" Finola waved it off. "She speaks to me, this ship, in her own language. It all blends together into words. Never mind that for now. You tell me how you think it all works."

It was a big question. Missy took a moment.

"The blades lift us up," she said. "Then we point up, or we point down, with the nose. And the ship follows."

"No, Missy. Not up and down. It's pitching..." Fin leaned forward on the main stick. The ship responded, nosing down. Then she pulled it toward herself, and the ship's nose rose once more.

"...rolling..." She twisted the same stick, and the ship banked, turning. She corrected, and it levelled straight again.

"...and yawing." She pushed a pedal with her foot. The ship slid on its axis, still moving forward but with a twist.

Missy gripped the armrests instinctively. "We're going forward, except we're sideways!"

"The rudder pedals, anti-torques, do that." The pilot took Missy's hand and placed it on the stick, her own hand wrapped around Missy's. "What you've got is the rudder, otherwise known as the cyclic—this controls our direction, pitch, and roll. The throttle—this lever—makes us go faster."

Clouds scattered, a bow wave. Then Finola let go. Missy held the stick firm, a vibration that fell somewhere between a tickle and numbness. *This is why she wears gloves.*

"I'm flying!" Missy whispered. Finola smiled.

"With that stick in your hand, you must think differently. Up here there is no forward or backward. No side-to-side. No up and down. We manoeuvre all these at once, like a dolphin in the deepest of seas. There is no single plane of existence for us. We dive and crest and tack and jibe. To pilot this ship is a multi-dimensional dance of wind and space."

Missy turned again to the stick gripped in her fist. She tilted slightly, barely a hair, as she'd seen Finola do. The nose lifted and the altitude meter clicked from 22,544 to 22,632.

"Getting our new recruit hooked on the throttle, fair pilot?" Rasmus stood at the cockpit door with one hand braced on the edge of it. He could see the girl's head, barely. He knew she couldn't see over the dashboard. No matter.

"Easy pickings," Finola replied, turning around to grin at her captain.

"See that she has some time on the rudder. Keep her up here a while." The girl was still unaware of his presence.

"Yes, Captain," she replied briskly, giving the child's shoulder a shake. "Captain's here."

The girl turned around and waved, her face alight, and the captain's face transformed in kind. He raised a fist of encouragement. "Well done, *flicka*! Life is good!"

She raised an answering fist before spinning round again in her seat. "Finola, tell me what this is. This screen with the straight line. It moves whenever I nose up or—pitch or yaw, I mean. What is it?"

"Watch it, Missy. It tells you if you're heading up or down when you can't see for weather. Always trust that line. Stay true to this screen, and that one—they keep you safe, port and starboard, fore and aft..."

Rasmus backed out of the cockpit, latching the door shut behind him. The girl herself would pitch, yaw, and roll on this path. She was bound to.

"Captain." A voice, low and urgent. He turned. It was Dutch. He'd been looking for him.

"What is it?"

The engineer raised a newspaper. As Rasmus reached for it, Dutch summarized.

"It's Trans-North. They've called the RCMP, and they're trying to speed up construction."

The headline read:

OIL COMPANY PLANS EXPANSION DESPITE SABOTEURS

"They had blueprints up at the press conference. They're trying to reach the U.S. border by fall, just as you projected, through the watershed. And through Blackfoot territory and three other towns, and too close to the nature preserve..."

The captain frowned, scanning the article.

The pipeline, one of the largest in history in both diameter and reach, will flow from northern Alberta through the U.S. heartland and down to the Gulf Coast refineries of Texas, and is a broader referendum on the oil sands industry itself. Further still, it may help decide North America's energy future.

"That's not all, Captain. Read the end."
The paper crumpled in his grip.

Trans-North, partnering with Econo-Line of the United States, plans a grid of four more pipelines to connect with the Alberta network as soon as the southern prairie line is completed. At a press conference, Trans-North spokesperson Nigel Edmond responded to questions about how recent sabotage will affect development. "Unchecked criminal activity will not and cannot stop progress," he said. "Repeated destruction of our equipment is unlawful, and threatens the economic growth of this province."

The ship lurched, sliding downhill, and a delighted shriek sounded from behind the cockpit door. Rasmus braced himself. Then Fin laughed, and the Avenger righted.

"Progress," Dutch growled, his head bent in towards his captain's. "Mega-pipelines connecting to mega-pipelines. Unchecked greed."

"Not unchecked." Rasmus pushed the newspaper back into the hands of his first mate and thundered down the hallway for his charts.

•••

YOU HAVE A COLLECT CALL FROM <*Eric, it's Eric, hurry u*—>. PRESS ONE TO ACCEPT THE CHARGES. The phone beeped.

"Hey, isn't your flight—"

Eric leapt in before his father had a chance. "I lost the cellphone charger, so listen. I think she might be after the Griffons, and the union stuck something to her pack when she went to headquarters, a GPS or something, and they're tricking her, and if she finds the Griffons they'll think she set them up and she did, I guess, but she doesn't know it and who knows where she is and even if we did, what are we going to do?"

The words came out in a tumble, as words tend to during desperate moments over sticky handsets. His father replied.

"We got another moth, Eric. We were right. She found them. She's on the Griffons' ship."

"Does she know the union knows?" Eric cried. "Does she know they're setting her up?"

"Doesn't look like it—"

Eric held the payphone with a shaking hand as a voice broadcast into the departures hall. AIR CANADA FLIGHT 696 FROM WINNIPEG TO HALIFAX BOARDING NOW AT GATE 24.

"Dad, I have to go. Tell Joe, tell everybody. I'm on my way home."

The line clicked and went dead. Dan Stewart hung up the kitchen phone gently, turning to his wife and his longtime friend, who looked at him anxiously for news.

"Radio for Hector, Sam, and Vince. Get them back here now. We need a plan."

Chapter Fifteen

THE CHASE

Correspondence from watchful eyes, newspaper clippings, and the view from 5,000 feet up charted a campaign of the most decisive damage. The Avenger was a blur of landings and liftoffs, and a few stolen hours of solid footing—never more than a day or so—was as prized as answers to questions the crew knew well enough not to ask. *When the captain has a plan, the captain will say so*, they said.

During one of those grounded moments somewhere in Northern Manitoba, Missy, twenty-seven rungs up an unfurled chain ladder, tightened her grip as a gust of wind sent her swaying and bumping against the hull. She felt a knock through the metal and looked up. Taro was there, waiting at the top. *Keep climbing*, he waved, and she did until he reached out a hand, and she took it. She swung her body up over the top and stood still as Taro clipped her carabiner onto the main line.

"You are safe," he said, with a light tug on the rope. "Sit."

Every surface conducted the chill in the air. The wind whipped her hair around her face. She tucked it behind her ears fruitlessly.

"It's higher up than I thought." She looked at the pirates moving far below, readying yet another beacon camp for one night on the ground.

"Yes," he replied cheerfully, digging in his tool belt. Taro circled the fuselage's roof with light feet, hopping from one feature to the next with the grace and precision of a cat. *Of course*. Missy thought of his nickname.

"Feathering shafts. Servo gears." He spoke slowly, turning to her and extending a hand to showcase each piece. "Pitch hinge. Teeter hinge. Scissor link and counterweight. Swashplates."

Missy nodded, blinking in the sun.

"And here…" He ran a gloved hand across the length of one, reaching high up above his head. "My custom blades. Nothing else like them in the world."

She looked up at four-pointed stars in silhouette, deceptively simple ribbons of metal that were highly designed. Taro had curved every edge to aerodynamic perfection, she knew. He waited for her to turn back to him before continuing.

"There are sixteen, four sets of four, as you see. Mechanized flaps cut through air more easily. We are a whisper of three or four decibels. A trained ear might pick up our turbine whine, but to the untrained and unexpecting, we are a breath of wind rustling curtains. Then we are gone."

How Phezzie, machinist with Missy's home crew, would gawk at all this. Sam, too. In the echo of the Dreads' burly and uncontained roar, the Griffons were cultured to the point of refinement. Yet Missy felt in her gut that one would deeply respect the other.

"Taro, are there pirates in Japan?"

"How does lift work?"

"How did you get all the way here?"

"What's that tool? What's that one?"

"Why are they this shape?"

"Have you ever crashed?"

For the rest of the afternoon he obliged her, padding lightly back and forth across the hull and its wings. He told her of flight dynamics and wind shifts, near-collisions and legendary pilots, of his childhood in Osaka.

"Like silk in the mouth," he said, sighing deeply as he fixed a socket wrench onto a bolt and cranked it loose. "Unagi, the great eel, snake of the sea. I miss it most. Cut by Chef Morika, it melts in your mouth. We find freshwater eel, now and then, you know. A few of them have grown quite the taste for it, even though it's nothing to Morika's."

He told her of the Bozu, the youngest pirate crew in the world, with their hovercraft ship and network of hidden caves.

"Their captain, Wikawa, is the most natural-born water pilot I've ever seen. Just as good as our Fin. He slips from water to land like a fog, and he's gone again just that quick. It's a bonanza in Japan. Packed with electronics and technological things. The people hardly notice when our brethren skim the fat. Japanese pirates have a refined taste in junk."

He told her of the Griffons' patch repairs and wing stability, de-icing and blizzards and blind landings. And he told her of his infamous fall that had prompted new rules of harnesses for

all on the high deck, and showed her the scar where the bone of
his leg had broken through the skin.

"Two stories down, you know. No slip to take lightly." He
chuckled. "That day I earned my name. The Cat. Didn't land on
my feet. A funny bunch, they are."

She stayed up there until well past dusk, bracing one thing as
he wrenched its counterpart, or handing him a fresh bolt or the
blowtorch or a spare length of electrical wire. Finally, the sun
long doused, he dismissed her with a spare nod.

"I'll need to sandblast the aft blades before the week is out,"
he said. "Your help would be good."

Missy made her way back down the ladder and across the
field with *Your help would be good* reverberating satisfactorily
through her mind. She bounded through the soddie door where
Ginsberg, Billy, and Birdie sat at the long table. Birdie smiled, as
always, and Billy and Ginsberg looked up from cards.

"Who's winning?" Missy swung one leg and then the other
across the bench and sat down.

"I am," said Ginsberg.

"Are not," said Billy, and Ginsberg scowled. "Where've you
been, kid?"

"Up on deck," she said, still flushed. "Helpin' Taro."

"Wha? Nah. You still got yer ears." Billy grinned from behind
his cards. "He talks 'em clear off."

"Cut it out, Grundy," Ginsberg said. "He's teasin' you, kid.
Cat don't say boo. Zipped up tight, he is, just like your Ike back

east. Damn near genius but not much for chattin'. Don't take it personal. Grundy, you're up."

Billy slapped a card onto the table and Ginsberg howled, defeated. Birdie, sitting with her hands wrapped around a steaming mug, caught Missy's eye.

"Didn't say boo?" she mouthed, one eyebrow raised. Missy shook her head and the two girls, bonded in an appreciation of Japanese metalwork, smiled.

• • •

"If someone could, you know. Only hear muffled and not much more. She lip-reads but really, she's…you know. Mostly deaf."

The floors in the pharmacy were too shiny, the fluorescents too bright, the piped-in music too chipper. He exhaled, loosening his scowl. *Come on, man. You can tolerate thirty thousand feet with a plugged pressure valve. You can tolerate this.*

"Mostly deaf?" The pharmacist coughed, clearing his throat. "Could be any number of things. Guess if it were me, I'd try turning up the volume and see if that helps."

The man in the white coat reached out to spin a display of reading glasses.

"These here, for example—five bucks and they'll make everything bigger. People don't always care about their diplopia or their hyperopia or the myopia. They just want to be able to read the paper. And so, for her, there's no harm in making everything louder. It won't be perfect. She might not have the right parts to hear. Some don't. It might be like putting a Band-Aid on a broken leg. But—maybe it would help. Who knows?"

"How much?"

The pharmacist moved behind the counter and presented Rolf with a small box from the shelf. "$269.99."

"That's a lot."

"It's the Songbird Ultra. Ultra-flexible, ultra-tonal, audiotronic…the only other one we have is the Magni-2000. It's plastic, but it'll do pretty much the same thing. It's $19.99."

From his pockets Rolf pulled a twenty-dollar bill and two toonies for the tax. He nodded tersely to the man in the white coat and walked to the exit door, pushing it with one hand. With the other, he tucked the box into his pocket where it stayed safe for a while, until it wasn't.

• • •

Dear Eric. September 22

Sorry its been a while. The Griffons were low on moths. Plus I'm flying. They're letting me train as a co pilot. Did you know you can make jet fuel out of onion rings?

Missy

P.S. I don't know when I'll be home. I'll tell you more later, if I make the letter too long it'll weigh down the moth and suck all the battery.

FLYGPOST P.P.S. Please don't say anything if the chief calls looking for me. I can't tell you why. Just don't.

• • •

"I'll call the police, I will! You wait!"

They'd all heard the doors of the truck open and slam shut. But then a shriek had rung out from the Stewarts' yard. *What was that?* A crush of bodies leapt to feet and pressed through the doorway to the yard. A man stood blinking in the sun, yelling at Ike.

"Don't you dare shove at me! Where am I? Say something! No! I don't want to go in there! I'm not going anywhere until you tell me—"

"ENOUGH!" Hector pressed his way through to Ike, who held the man's arm firmly, his truck keys dangling. "Brute. What is all this?"

Ike, in a state of calm that made no sense next to the agitation of the unknown man, let go to grasp an identification badge from the man's front pocket. He yanked and it popped off. He handed it to Eric.

"Hey!" the man cried. "Give that back."

Eric read from the badge. "Neil MacDonald. It says here he's a doctor."

The man straightened, indignant.

"My man Ike is well-meaning but perhaps rough in his execution." Hector took the badge from Eric, and glanced briefly. "Let us all be patient so we may understand why he felt it necessary to bring you to us."

The man glowered.

"Please, come inside." Eric's father ushered the small crowd back into the house. "There's no point in us all being out here when the tea is steeped."

With everyone reassembled, the man sat at the kitchen table, twitching nervously. Hector sat across from him.

"Dr. Neil MacDonald. Tell us how you came to be in the company of our man Ike, as he cannot."

After an exasperated pause, the man spoke.

"I was getting into my car in the parking lot of the lecture hall. I'd finished a talk on applications of enzymes and substrates in bio-reactor design. I was about to go to my lab but then he"—he pointed at Ike—"blocked my way and handed me this."

The professor unfolded a crumpled piece of paper and laid it on the table. *FOLOW ME ORE ELSE. PLEEZ* was scrawled in stolen pencil.

"I said I would absolutely not. That's when he grabbed me"—his volume increased—"and pushed me into his truck! Not a word of explanation, and he drove me here. You will hear from my lawyer."

"Thank you, sir, for telling us how it went." Hector turned to Ike. "Why?"

Ike pointed at the ID badge in Eric's hands as though the reason should be plain. Hector looked at Eric, an unspoken order, and the boy read it out loud.

"Dr. Neil MacDonald, PhD. Professor in Avionics and

Biochemical Engineering, Dalhousie University...?"

"Oh, Ike." After days of failed ideas and frantic brainstorms, Joe stepped into the light with a broad smile on his face. "Clever Ike."

Chapter Sixteen

MONKEYWRENCH

"*Just* milk. No sugar."

Eric crossed the room with a steaming mug and placed it in front of Dr. MacDonald. "Here you go, professor."

Apologies made, the task of consulting had begun. *We need you*, Joe had explained. *Just an hour or two.*

As much of an asset as he was to his field, the professor's expertise was a very narrow one that generated few urgent requests. He took a sip of tea and sat back in the chair, surveying the kitchen and its occupants, enjoying that powerful moment between questions asked and answers given.

"This is hypothetical to the point of ridiculous," he said, putting down his mug. "Biofuels are not a new idea, but there's a ceiling there, you see. We scientists hit our heads on this ceiling very quickly. If we could make jets fly with even a small concentration of biofuels, we would save millions. Billions. Resources. Ticket prices. Emissions. It would change everything. But the trouble is the very thing you can't avoid, with a jet."

"What's that?" Sam leaned forward. The conversation was veering toward his stomping ground—unsolvable problems.

"Altitude," the professor said. "With every thousand feet you rise above the ground, the temperature drops two degrees. If it's a nice spring day in Halifax—and it's, say, eighteen degrees—it's only sixteen degrees a thousand feet above Halifax. And fourteen degrees two thousand feet up. And so on."

Reggie yawned. The professor continued, unbothered.

"Ten thousand feet up and it's two degrees below zero. Commercial jets fly more than three times that high. Even in the summer, it's freezing up there. That's why jet fuels are so costly. They're formulated so they'll never freeze."

Joe paced the kitchen mindful of the growing significance of all this. "Say someone invents an aviation biofuel that won't freeze."

"Algae. Corn derivatives. Plant-based. They've tried it all."

"What about biofuel made with…" Joe cleared his throat. "… cooking oil?"

The man snorted. "People make grease gas in their backyards for old station wagons," he said. "We're talking about multi-million dollar jets."

"I know. Humour me, professor." Joe stopped pacing to stand at the head of the table.

"All right." He sighed. "See, biofuel from cooking grease is the most crude of all alternative sources. If someone could make it work for jets—the most complicated vehicle in the most demanding environment—that person would unlock the mystery of making all kinds of biofuels work in all kinds of vehicles. Pollution would be cut in half. Travel would be revolutionized. It would be a huge economic boom—a sustainable one, as long as we don't go messing it up by turning fields that grow food into fields that grow fuels. We waste a lot of effort and space right now. If we were smart, I think we could do it. Like anything else, it's a balance. If we can figure out that balance, biofuels are the single most profitable scientific discovery to be made. And it is yet unmade."

He rattled along without regard for anyone keeping up, but enough was clear. There were no more yawns. He concluded by stating what had already become apparent.

"The person to invent a biofuel that could run efficiently in commercial airliners—that person would be the richest scientist ever known."

"Riches? Feh." Sam was derisive, as Sam tended to be. Hector sat with his chin in his hands, engrossed in the flicker of a candle.

"You'd be hard pressed to find anyone who'd choose not to be rich, Sam." Dan Stewart chuckled, but coughed and went quiet at the look on Sam's face. The gunner stood up and took steps back from the table where everyone sat. Then he turned around, his palms facing out.

"Look at my boots." Everyone looked. "When it rains the wet comes in one end and drains out the other. If it weren't for duct tape I'd be workin' in my sock feet."

Derisiveness was common. Speechmaking was not, and Sam had assumed the position.

"I'd like me a set of fresh boots. I'd like blades an' drivers an' wrenches that haven't got bites taken out of 'em, that don't shoot sparks. I wouldn't run indoors if it started snowin' twenties. But what do I need? A bed stuffed o' feathers? What's that you call that stuff, miss? Cream of bru-lee with all that sugar on top and sauce with the caramel on a brassy spoon with a picture of the Queen fixed onto it? Someone taggin' along after me sayin'"— (he raised his voice to a falsetto)—"*Yes, Sam!* and *No, Sam!* and *Don't You Look Fine Today, Sam!*"

A lone snort erupted.

"Look at Reggie." He pointed to the pantry where the jury-rigger stood chewing on the end of a finger. "I've seen that man in creased pants. Skunk in a ballgown."

Reggie, ever the good sport, bowed deeply to a round of whooping.

"We pilot the most wicked ship in all the woods." Sam grew louder. "We have our food. Our junk. What we make, what we grow, what we take. We have space and air and work. Folk what want riches? Birds in cages. Sittin' there till they rot. Not knowing how to do nuthin' fer themselves. Lookin' clever. Not bein' clever. Never seein' the guts o' nuthin."

He paused for effect and sniffed haughtily. "I'd like boots. But money an' trappins'? I'll have none of it. And I'll eat my own head if one 'o you pirates disagrees."

A mug clattered to the floor.

"Pirates?" cried Professor Neil MacDonald.

•••

Meanwhile, on the Avenger, Cirrus's boot had been made
viscous with a spill of hydraulics fluid on the hold floor. The
note, in an unfortunate lurch of turbulence, had dislodged from
the front pocket of Missy's pack. It fell, feather-like, to the floor
as his sister, the machinist, walked past.

"There's paper on you."

He lifted one foot and Birdie pulled at the piece of grease-
smudged white. As she read, her face sank. She looked at the
cockpit, to where Rasmus was bent in counsel with Fin, then
back to her brother, the note still in her hand.

"What? What is it?"

"She…the apprentice…" Her eyes filled up, first with
confusion and then with anger.

"She what? What is it, Birdie?"

She gripped the paper tightly in her fist. "I need the captain.
Now."

•••

"What is it?" Missy sniffed, poking at the mound on her plate
with a fork. It sprang back, coarse and a little fragrant. The
engine rumbled up through their feet, the table, and through
mugs and plates, a constant vibration to which she had become
accustomed.

"Stewed moss." Jesper filled a spoon and tipped it back with
broth, chewing, then wiping his mouth on his sleeve. "Cooked
with lots of salt and butter. Pip grows it in greenhouses along

with beets and herbs and everything else. We've got a greenhouse at beacon 14, two smaller ones at beacon 26, and the biggest one is at beacon 8. You've only seen the one at 14, I think."

Missy stirred and lifted some to her mouth, Jesper watching her with a friendly look and a nod. It was much like Joe's beet greens but chewier and fuzzier, with an earthy, deeply green flavour.

"There's garlic in there," she said. "It's delicious."

"What's that, Miss-you?" Pip, passing with a tray, winked.

"Delicious!"

"Well, of course it is!" Pip swayed between the benches, picking up and laying down new things. Missy, watching her, thought about gypsies and good witches.

"Who tends all the greenhouses?" She looked at Jesper.

"We have…" He looked over one shoulder, then the other. "…friends."

"The Bloods?"

"Them and others like them."

"BULLSEYE!"

Jesper reacted, turning toward the stern doors, then back to Missy. "They're calling you."

She followed his gaze and saw Cam beckoning at her, a thick coil of rope over his shoulder. She dropped her fork with a clatter and rose, climbing over the bench and thrusting one boot on and the next. The ship had begun a descent. Something was about to happen.

"I like that moss, Pip," she called. "See you later, Jailbird."

She tumbled through the mess and out the double hatch to the freight hold, her boots clopping unevenly until they hooked her heels.

"Here I am." The girl's eyes were bright.

She is acclimatized. Good thing. The ship's windmaster handed her a harness. "Step into this."

His urgency made her heart thump. She reached for the woven straps and pulled the harness over each leg and around her waist. Cam stepped circles around her, cinching and pulling. Ginsberg, splayed on the floor with his face pressed to thick Plexiglas, looked up.

"It's dark but clear enough to see. There's no activity on the road. We're clear."

"Green light for wrench," Cam called to Rolf, and Rolf called to Magnus, and Magnus called to Fin. The ship hovered lower than Missy had ever seen without landing, the tops of trees flailing wildly at the force of the ship. Cam knelt in front of her.

"Listen, girl." He put his hands on her shoulders. "The pipeline company's about to drop another length of snake, and you know Captain. Snake gets right up in his craw."

He clipped a metal carabiner around the loop at her waist.

"See this?" He grabbed a thick steel loop fixed to the floor of the ship. He tugged it. "This is tested to four thousand pounds."

From the corner of her eye Missy saw Brock push closed the hatch to the rest of the ship, sealing it. Cam clipped another carabiner into the anchoring loop and wove the rope through it, then through a hoist he held in his hands, with every movement looking intently at her as if to say *See? Safe.* The rope attached to her was attached to the ship. He called to Brock.

"Open the hatch." A rush of night wind filled the hold and he turned to her again. "The construction site is down there, by that river."

He led her to the porthole in the floor, her harness and its fixtures clinking as she walked. A broad swath of water twisted through the forest just beneath the ship, churned into whitecaps by the proximity of the ship.

"They've laid cradles and they've brought in a crane. All that's left is the pipe and the poison. It's too wooded for a landing. Do you understand, Missy?"

She looked at Cam. There was a sheen of nerves over his face, but his eyes were steady. She looked through the open hatch to the expanse of black sky that waited for her to drop into it. She nodded. While Cam took his position at the hoist, Brock ushered her forward.

"Take these." He handed her a set of loppers and a broad-barrelled flashlight. "Cam is going to lower you down. When you hit the ground we'll give you slack on the rope and then you're going to unclip and disable the crane. You'll cut the hydraulics and the lines that run up the boom. It'll delay construction long enough for us to catch up from the other side, thirty kilometres south of Stand Off."

She nodded again, pushing her hair out of her face. The wind yanked it loose again.

"Missy—we don't like oilmen. Oilmen don't like us." He secured the loppers to her belt. "If you see any sign of anyone, signal up and we'll get you out of there. We're quiet for a rotor ship, thanks to Taro's blades. But not quiet enough when we're this close to the ground. Get down quick and get up quicker."

"How high up are we?"

"Two hundred and fifty-three feet." It was not Brock who answered, but Rasmus, who stepped into Missy's view suddenly as though he'd been watching all along. He looked very stern. He moved toward her deliberately, each step measured, his arms crossed in front of his chest. He paused in front of her without flinching at the outside.

"Thirty feet or five thousand, *flicka*, and you'd crack yourself if you fell either way. Are you with us, apprentice?"

Missy nodded, unsettled more by the expression on his face than the 253 feet. From across the bay, Cam shook the rope to get her attention. She turned to him.

"I've got you," he mouthed, his fist wrapped tight around the hoist.

He's done this before. For him I'm a feather. She looked back to where Rasmus Krook had been standing. He was gone.

Brock nudged her forward beyond the safe point, anchored into a rope himself just in case. "Sit here," he yelled now, perched at the edge of metal as the ship hovered over target.

Finola's voice rang out over the intercom, unheard by Missy except for the effect of it upon the others. Brock patted her back and Cam steadied himself, both hands on the hoist. It was time.

Under the ship's lights, she could see a cluster of dormant trucks and the crane, the mother of the snake. Missy would cripple it. She closed her eyes. She thought about Vince's banjo and the ghost in love with the water-fetching girl of Caney Fork. She thought about apple trees and salt, hurricanes and garrison forts, the warm-pipe scent of Joe's flannel shirt. She wondered if Eric's old bike was where she'd left it, leaning against the canoe in the barn. She wondered if Eric was where she'd left him. All this in the flash of seconds before she felt one final assertion state itself inside her mind:

I'd never want to be ordinary anyway.

She pushed herself over the edge and into a cyclone.

Chapter Seventeen

THE WRECK OF THE AVENGER

Missy's throat constricted in instinctive panic, eyes clamped shut at first, clutching desperately at the rope that held her weight and her life. Once the shock of pushing off the edge had eased, she opened her eyes as well as she could, squinting against the wind, and went limp. What else was there to do, after all? She was entirely reliant on the harness, the quality of its webbing, the carabiner locks, the weave of the rope, Fin's steady hover and Cam's hands on the other end, calloused and knobbly. *They use these lines in the Himalayas, you know, when they climb Everest*, he'd said. *Strongest there is.* She wondered if this is what made her uneasy—reliance upon others, as she was accustomed to relying mostly on herself—or if it was the 253 feet, or the captain's unusual mood.

She gulped another breath and looked up at the belly of the ship and Taro's rotors spinning above it. Brock was there, pushed out as far as he could, leaning on his own rope, craning to keep his eyes on her. Then she could feel the mist and smell the mud of the riverbank. Over the water she swayed violently with a gust of wind and the ship rocked. She swayed, holding on.

Suddenly, there were pebbles under her feet and she crumpled, landing in a heap. She righted herself urgently to the memory of her father's voice.

You'll feel my smile through the darkest black.

• • •

"Cockpit to bay, cockpit to bay, come in, bay. Pick up, over." Fin's voice carried over the radio.

"Bay here." Brock, still watching for Missy through the open door, answered the call.

"Is she on the ground, over?"

"Ten-four, the girl is away," Brock replied. "Got my eyes on her right now. Why?"

There was no answer. The ship lurched again, then the radio crackled.

"There's been an explosion on the horizon. We have to get out of here. Now."

"CAM!—" Brock shouted.

With a pop, the rope went slack. Smoke rose to the north. On the ground, the speck of a girl signalled with her flashlight—flash-flash—the midnight equivalent of a raised fist. She had unclipped.

• • •

The moon was plenty bright enough, once her eyes adjusted. It was a pretty river, broad and edged with trees that draped over eddies and pools. A crude road had been built, and trucks sat idle in a clearing next to the water. She ran across the landscape to the crane's haunches and began to climb, scrambling along an outrigger to the operator's compartment, then from the roof to the lattice boom. She could see her target now—a series of wires that ran several stories to the top of the machine, and the guy line, the pulley rope. She began to climb—not unlike climbing an apple tree, but colder and rustier, and with man-made footholds.

SNIP. The loppers were sharp. With a *sproing* the first hydraulic wire went slack. Missy opened the loppers again and repeated all the way across the boom, then the pulley rope, then the guy line. It floundered, hanging on by the last wire, the thickest. *SNIP* and the whole thing gave way. She shimmied back down to the roof of the cab, then leapt from the outriggers to the ground, kicking a tire for good measure. *I did it! I stopped the—*

The rope hit the ground beside her. She looked up. Brock, almost too distant to make out, was signing *UP.* Missy wondered why, but clipped in to an immediate yank that lifted her off her feet. The loppers dropped from her hands and clattered onto the rocks. Cam was hoisting frantically, faster than he'd lowered her. The ship had already started to move, dragging her through the sky. Brock was shouting and pointing. An onslaught of light broke through into the clearing, a line of one-ton trucks skidding to a stop where the dirt road landed at the shore. Doors sprang open and angry, coveralled men jumped out, gaping furiously at the ship and at the only perpetrator they could clearly discern—Missy.

In the commotion, she'd almost forgotten to leave the note. She fumbled in her chest pocket and dropped it, watching it tumble end over end until it landed and was picked up by one of the oil men.

HAVE AN UPLIFTING DAY. ~ G

Missy's smile faded as she looked up to the belly of the ship, then to a column of flame and smoke rising on the horizon. *What the—*

CRACK! The ship weaved suddenly and Missy winced with the pressure, the harness straining against the velocity of evasive manoeuvres. The force of the rotors reverberated through her body now, and she fought against the wind to keep her eyes open.

POP. POP POP CRACK!

She looked up, confused—had she heard that, or felt it? A metallic stench reached her nose and just there, in the hull above her head: a smoking bullet hole.

Guns. They've got guns!

She shrieked, pulling her legs up instinctively. Brock yelled back through the bay, urging Cam to hurry, then he locked all his attention on Missy. *Good girl, hang on.* Above her, Rolf and Grundy had sprinted to the hold to lay more muscle onto the rope, and they heaved in unison. The shade of the ship settled over her and hands grasped her harness, yanking her up and dropping her onto the floor. She saw Brock's grizzled jaw as he bellowed, "SHUT THE HATCH!"

Grundy, across the bay, yelled "ALL CLEAR!" into his radio as the ship banked sharply and they were away, safe, or so it seemed.

•••

"What happened? Who were they? There was fire!" Missy shouted through the commotion, eyes darting for one face or another, for anyone who might answer her. They all pushed and shoved, frantic for their stations, and so she climbed through the hatch with Cam at her front and Brock at her back, all of them pushing through the ship for the captain.

He looked up from a table spread with charts, his face twisted in stress. The ship banked again and they all paused, grabbing hold as the Avenger climbed higher. Then his hands were on her shoulders, his face level with hers.

"*Flicka.*" He tried and failed to mask the strain behind his eyes. "Well done."

•••

Pages from CHAPTER IV: EMERGENCY PROCEDURES, from *Flight Dynamics: Rotor Art & Science* flashed into Missy's mind. *During mechanical engine failure, pilots may use the stored energy from the spinning propellers to get one last boost of lift right before the vessel hits the ground, softening impact.*

It had started with a sputter, a backup of a backup failing. A fuel tank had been punctured by bullets. A flashing red light in the cockpit and a shudder and then pirates shoved one another aside to reach stations and safety belts and one mechanical failure triggered another and then it had all gone wrong, wholly and completely. Missy sprinted up front, still harnessed, darting through clusters of shouting pirates as the blades gulped for air, pitching the fuselage wildly.

From the cockpit, one hand on the stick, Fin turned and screamed over her shoulder, her hair whipping round her face, the pilot's chair bucking underneath her.

"CAPTAIN! PERMISSION TO AUTOROTATE!"

Missy watched as Rasmus staggered from the nav station to the windshield, one hand in the air in wordless agreement.

Rapidly varying airspeeds and blade angles present a difficulty in predicting aerodynamics during autorotation.

With one fist gripped to a net of webbing, Missy braced herself, feet in a wide stance, the ship now a hopelessly heavy, metal thing that hung lifeless in mid-air.

Skilled changes to the collective and cyclic pitch are necessary during the manoeuvre to manage the energy of the rotor and the airspeed of the craft.

Control panels all over the ship shrieked alarms of failure that she felt through the soles of her boots. The ship was a tantrum. She wondered if this was how it felt in the blue whale's belly in the angriest northeasterlies, when the ocean roiled up and turned everything upside-down. Her stomach lurched. *Daddy.*

"READY CAPTAIN!" Fin threw a desperate call over her shoulder. "THERE'S A FIELD—"

He yelled back, bracing at the neck of the cockpit. "*NER PÅ MARKEN!*"

Finola pulled back hard on the stick as the engine stalled. Replacing its roar was a strange silence, only the strain of bolts and the creaking of metal things pushing and pulling against one another, and the howling of wind, and the dizzying sensation of spinning, unpropelled, through a storm.

"*RAAAAGGGGGHHHH!*" The veins in the master pilot's throat snaked down her neck as she cried out, pushing with all her weight on the stick, and the turbine screamed. The moment imprinted indelibly upon the last, for the time being, of Missy's consciousness.

• • •

The stillness that followed the crash was more startling than the crash itself. Sober elation and composed shock and dazed clarity and many other sensations that made no sense. Missy raised her head and winced at the ache, raising her hand to feel a bump. *Am I on the floor? The ceiling?* Tilted sharply, she rolled down and righted herself, her arms braced against the hull and the floor, now a steep hill. She stepped down the length of the fuselage wall toward the freight door, through which she could see a crack of dawn's light. There were other bodies too, shuffling, coming to. She called out as she made her way.

"Cirrus! Mag! Taro?"

One by one they answered her, a roll call of sorts, though she could only register those who stumbled toward her, or who tapped in response on the metal she touched. She reached the hatch door, which had been crushed. She saw wet grass through it and sat down, wiggling her legs out first, torn metal tugging at her. She landed in the dirt. Rolf was there, and others beyond him. He looked at her urgently.

"Are you whole, *flicka*?"

"I am not in pieces." She giggled. Rolf frowned. "No. I mean, yes. I cracked my head but I'm good. You asked me if I was a hole. That makes no sense, Wolf. No sense at all."

She looked past the coxswain, who eyed her with concern. Cam and Brock, who had both caught up to her, were speaking to her but she could not focus. Her head spun. She saw Cirrus stumble by, calling for his sister. She saw Shivers, blurred. She blinked twice. The navigator was talking to Rolf.

"Southwest of Cold Lake, Saskatchewan. We go west on foot…"

Then her legs gave out. Then a beard in her face, dark eyes peering out through wiry black. She pushed on the ground.

"Easy. You are not yourself." Rolf scooped her up and began to walk, carrying her through grasses that reached his waist.

"We fell! We fell from the sky." *Why can't I stop chattering? I can't stop chattering.* "If I'm a hole, am I empty, or full? I like holes. They're good for hiding…"

Missy looked up. In the night sky beyond the underside of the pirate's bristled chin, stars peeked through the clouds and there it was. The great blue whale broached the grey and soared toward her. She blinked. It grinned wide, baring its baleen. A woman's voice called out to her as though through cupped hands.

Hallooo, my princess! There you are!

The whale swooped out of her frame of sight, then dove back away from the dawn and was gone.

"Here I am," she murmured. Against Rolf's chest she felt the vibration of his voice. Her dangling feet swayed in time with his every step. "You're saying something. I wish I could hear it."

It began to rain. Then the world went black around the edges until her eyelids fluttered shut.

•••

Rolf shushed the girl kindly, though she didn't know, her head lolling over his forearm. He bent sideways as he carried her, assessing his own damage. The wound had eviscerated the left leg of his pants clear through the pocket, what was left of it shredded against bruised and bloodied skin. His thank-you to her for her postcard—which he carried with him everywhere he went—was gone. A bit of sound, it might have been, now lost. He turned one more time toward the wreck, crumpled metal hissing and smoldering in the grass, then looked down at the young apprentice in his arms.

We wish for all kinds of things. But we don't need all kinds of things. You hear me fine, Missy Bullseye.

•••

For what felt like hours he carried her, his gait lulling her in and out of consciousness. He'd wrapped her in a blanket but every now and then her feet would brush tall grass and the wetness of it would jolt her back into awareness. *There was a fire. They had guns. Guns! We crashed.* Other figures walked alongside, arms laden with whatever camp stock and food and overnight supplies they'd salvaged from the wreck of Avenger. Rolf slowed, and Missy willed herself to consciousness.

"There was smoke. What was the smoke?"

"Not now. Later," he replied.

"I can walk," she murmured. Rolf, not inclined to fussing, set her down gently on her feet and crouched with his hands on her shoulders like a weeble-wobble doll.

"Good?" he said, appraising her.

"Fine," she replied. "I'm fine, Rolf."

She broke free from his grasp to do a little jig, and he chuckled.

"Right then, *flicka*. Off you go."

The effort had made her head spin. She ached all over, her ears ringing from the inside out with concussion, but she didn't want to be carried anymore. In the darkness she was swept along with a tide of feet through the grass, asking now and then to lighten the loads of others, but they all refused with tired smiles.

"No need," panted Billy, bent under the weight of Pip's supply sacks. "Go and see how much longer, will yeh?"

She walked faster, though unsteadily, needing the kick of it. She was grateful for the ground under her feet and enlivened by occasional splashes of mud. As she neared the front line of the mob they all congested, a pileup climbing through a grove of trees and up the ditch of a dirt road. Missy broke through between Cirrus, who carried three duffels, and Shivers, who carried an armful of weatherproof satchels protecting her maps. They had reached a wall.

"A wall," she said, unnecessarily. The road ended at a small parking lot and an old fortification made of stone. There was a door and a sign engraved in weathered brass: NORTHWEST MOUNTED POLICE 1878–1883. BATTLE CREEK BARRACKS. She looked at Cirrus questioningly.

"Fort Walsh," he mouthed through the rain. Missy saw relief on his face.

"Allow me." Taro stepped forward industriously, a small hammer in his hand, and bent to *tap-tap-tap* gently on each hinge. "We must not distress such a primitive bit of metalwork. But we must demand that it opens in the hopes that what lies beyond it is warm and dry."

He stepped back, water sloshing off the brim of his hat. "Two-Hands, Billy, if you please."

The brutes stepped forward, massive fingers poised on ribs of iron. Billy limped a little, the residual effect of some unstowed thing that had fallen on his leg in the melee. Missy shivered.

"On two," Ginsberg nodded. "One. Two."

The door popped off its hinges with a slight crack and the pirate crew spilled through, one by one, into a neat courtyard with horse stalls, supply sheds, lookout towers, and a large cabin.

All that and the modern fixtures of museum life: a concession stand, a mural of Mounties in formation, and, since the federal museum cuts of 1996, a PERMANENT CLOSURE sign along with a KEEP OUT notice from Parks Canada.

Grundy, with a gash on his forehead that seeped down the length of his face, slapped a bloodied hand against the window of the admissions booth.

"Ticket, please!" A five-dollar bill stuck there, sopping wet and smeared with red.

Those within earshot cracked up. Gwynne, carrying a pile of charts atop a bin of salvaged food, nudged Grundy's dropped payload with her foot.

"You're an animal." She grinned, her face in no better shape than his.

The rain had stopped. Missy looked up at the sky. A flag drooped at the top of a pole, a modified British Union Jack and ancestor of Canada's maple leaf. She passed under it as she stepped into a new day's shelter. *A flag means welcome, or stay away. I can't remember which.*

• • •

Not much functioned within the steaming, mangled guts of the Avenger, with the exception of one imperceptibly small device that noted a sudden stillness. Second by second, it counted down 48 hours to its duty—the transmission of its coordinates. A flash of intermittent red illuminated the embossed symbol on its casing: *T.H.U.G.S.S.*

Chapter Eighteen

THE INVASION OF BATTLE CREEK

"Brock, Find the fuse box. Ginsberg, give Pip a hand with food. See what you can find in the canteen. Birdie, dig up what you can for the fire."

Without stopping to shake off the wet, the pirates spread through the museum in a state of choreographed efficiency, a team anticipating duty without a need for orders. Battery-powered worklights, usually kept on board to signal from ship to ground, illuminated the search for paper, wood, kindling, candles. Before long a warm glow filled the old police outpost and from there, tables were laid with unwrapped food, the beginnings of supper. Water steamed to boiling in pots hung over the fire, boots in rows, wet gear hung upon the very same hooks that had once held proud red. Magnus, Finola, Taro, and Gwynne, owners of all the domains of flight, sat huddled at a small table, heads together. Missy sidled closer, straining through dim light for speculation on engine and rotors and velocity of impact.

"Without new blades, we are grounded." Taro shook his head. "Safe for now, far enough from guns. We flew a ways before the engine failed. Far enough so they don't know they hit us, and our eagle had the grace to fall in a spot that's far from any eyes. But we are grounded."

Magnus frowned. "We need more than blades. We need starboard hull facing, second section. We need metal."

A shove to her elbow and Missy startled. It was Jesper.

"You and me are on recovery," he said. "We need dry clothes. This way."

She followed the boy to the back of the room and down a dark hallway lined with framed pictures and tall glass cases. Jesper switched on a flashlight and Missy did the same, and faceless muslin figures appeared, dioramas, an unending watch stuffed to approximate the broad chests and bravery of the nation's first lawmen. Tall hats with stiff brims, red coats, badges and brass buttons, riding boots polished to shining. 1896–1898: Gold Rush Enforcers. 1891–1912: Guarding the Great Western Railway.

"There's a lock," Jesper stood in front of 1878–1883: Legacy of Battle Creek. Missy was already digging in the front pocket of her sweater. She pulled out her hand and held out her palm. It was a bobby pin. She slipped it into the lock and wriggled it. Jesper stepped back, deferring.

"Sorry, Railway. We need your jacket." She looked to the officer's left. "You too, Gold Rush."

Some time later the two staggered back down the hallway, barely able to see over heaps of red wool, leaving behind them a lineup of naked muslin.

•••

The pirate captain pressed himself against the alcove. At the other end of the hallway, Jesper and the girl rifled through display cases for dry clothes. Despite her questionable loyalty, the girl felt like his charge as much as the young boy, his best friend's son. Rasmus Krook, breath held, willed himself into shadow. His two smallest pirates muttered to one another, pleased, arms heaping, and disappeared again through the doors toward the main room.

I am not to be seen. Not like this.

The others would inventory their rattlings, nerves, and wounds together, but not he. He was their captain, indefatigable in defeat. *Nej, nej, nej, hela striden är förlorad…* The pipe would be laid, yet another battle lost, the suits and their brokers free to wreck and ruin. He slumped against the wall until his duty gently asserted itself once more in his mind.

A captain lost to despair is a captain lost to his crew.

He sighed, stood, and advanced toward the nearest glass case. He dabbed the yellowed cotton sleeve of a policeman, stale and dusty, across his face, one side at a time—blood, bruise, sweat, salt—then returned to his company as presentable as any of them. *Res upp.*

•••

Bloods:
Crashed October 4 on our way to
you after sighting a burst of
smoke along the lines.
Minor injuries. Ship in
grievous state. Grounded at
Fort Walsh. Please send news.
                — Sipiapo

FLYGPOST

Rasmus Krook rolled the paper tightly and slipped it into the
tube, twisting the lid tight. 2 KMS EAST OF BEACON 29:
STAND OFF. He programmed the console and shut it again,
switching the moth to flight mode. It awoke and fluttered
obediently in his palm. A breeze came up and he shuddered
in the doorway of the dusty holding cell, its only prisoner a
mannequin dressed as a lawless gold prospector.

"Fly, little one," he whispered. The moth glowed and whirred
from his hand, hanging there a moment above his head. "Raise
our friends."

He watched it as long as he could until it shrank into the
night.

"Captain," a voice called out from across the yard. "Sustenance."

"Indeed." He turned toward borrowed windows that glowed, for the time being, with improvised warmth.

•••

With bellies full and the fire radiating, a quiet settled over the barracks. Some were in quiet conversation while others collapsed on cots underneath newfound wool, surrendering to exhaustion. Missy sat against the stone wall, her knees up, watching sparks. Jesper was there too, stoking coals, wearing a jacket that went to his knees. Taro sat on a stool, hunched over a kit bag filled with an array of vicious-looking tools, removing each one gingerly to wipe it with a dry cloth. He looked up briefly, sensing Missy's gaze.

"Rust is no friend of hardworking metal."

Grundy hobbled toward them, wincing as he settled himself onto the bench next to Rasmus. He had a black eye, and the gash on his forehead had crusted over.

"What d'yeh say, fellas?" he grunted, wincing. "Oh, my freakin' knee."

"Rough bump today, Bill." Rasmus offered a hand and Grundy took it, nodding. "Rougher than in a long while."

The quiet settled over them again, tiredness and gratitude all mixed together, aches and hurts here and there, the Avenger turned upside down and all its crew in turn. Missy stood up.

"Can somebody tell me...what was the smoke?"

Magnus and Rolf, who'd been in counsel at the back of the room, turned from one another and moved forward. They were joined by Cam and Cirrus, who leaned along the wall to listen. Fin, looking worn, was the first to speak.

"We say *res upp* when we do what, Missy?"

"'Rise up.' That's the takeoff order."

"Indeed. But it is not only our takeoff—it is our calling. We *res upp* against wrongdoing. We follow our captain." She nodded in his direction. "But there is a commanding force higher than him—"

"Who's *her* higher commander?" A small but indignant figure sprang from the darkness. It was Birdie. She moved to stand in front of Missy, who stood as well, matching the welder's posture.

"Who's *your* boss?" Birdie repeated again, speaking her first words to Missy in a while. She stepped aggressively closer, hushing the room.

"Birdie Worthy." Krook's voice was measured.

"I brought this to you and you've done nothing," snipped the metalsmith at her captain. "I can't go any longer without knowing why she's here."

Rasmus tensed. "I already know why she is here."

"So do I," said Birdie, her eyes narrowing. "But I need her to say it out loud. So we all know."

He nodded his permission, and Birdie took a breath, turning to Missy.

"We saw your note, me and Cirrus. We showed the captain. The note you're going to send to the union. You're not with us. You're with them. You are a spy."

The room gasped, all eyes gone wide and fixed upon Missy. Taro, Ginsberg, Pip, Magnus. She scanned them all, frantic, until she reached Rolf, whose hand rested over his mouth in shock. He shook his head, turning away.

"Please, can everybody sit down? Look, I'll tell you. I'll tell you everything. With all of you standing up, I can't follow what you're saying." Missy swept with her hands, motioning for them all to settle opposite her. They shuffled and moved chairs and Missy stood with her back to one fire, her front to another.

Rasmus raised a palm in her direction. "You have the floor, *flicka*. I advise you to start at the beginning."

She did. She told them of everything that had foiled her probation. Avalanches in the Cariboos, earthquakes in the jungles of Ecuador, a busted submarine, a German drydock. She told them about wanting her own ship, and about the whale, the sea all glittering with diamonds for her mother, its queen, and her father, its king. She told them about the chief's shiny desk, and how her father had taught her to be hungry. She told them about the deal she'd reached to find the Griffons and aid in their apprehension in return for full status, or at least the start of it.

"That's you dealing your way in, not earning it," Birdie snapped.

Rolf rose to his feet, walked slowly through the frozen crowd, and pulled a stool up to sit in front of her. His scrutiny, given his kindness, made her eyes well up with shame. She hung her head. Still unspeaking, the wolf cocked his head, moppish and black, to order her gaze.

Is it true? He mouthed.

She said nothing, overwhelmed with shame. He eyed her firmly and spoke aloud.

"She has been with us longer than any spy would be. Long enough to get what she needed and be off by now."

They all went still for some time, digesting this one inarguable point. Missy finally spoke as much to him as to the room, and with more regret and sorrow than she'd ever felt in her life.

"When I told them I would find you, I didn't know you yet. I wasn't even sure when I wrote the—" Suddenly, the most obvious thing occurred to her. She spun around in search of her accuser, who stood opposite the captain, looking unconvinced. "Wait. Which note?"

Birdie scowled. "What do you mean?"

"Which note did you find?"

"The one where you told the union about us and said you'd help them find us, just like they told you to do."

Taro winced and drew breath through his teeth.

"I wasn't going to send that one, Birdie." Missy shook her head vigorously, speaking in a hurried tumble. "As soon as I found out about the monkeywrenching and all your work, with the fuel, the pollution… I mean, I thought I knew about pollution. But I didn't, did I? I worried about what to do, so I wrote two notes to see how each one would feel. I sent the one that felt the best. I sent them lookin' for wild geese."

Missy turned back to Birdie who listened, her face confused and shaking. Her brother rose.

"She saw our spirit, Birdie. Can't you see? She was a union spy, but then she turned. She turned for us."

Birdie looked from her brother to her captain and back again before pulling a battered piece of paper from her pocket and handing it to Missy, who held it a while in her open palm. She saw the muck of a boot sole and pieces of words through tears. Looking up to the young metalsmith, she crumpled the note and threw it over her shoulder, pitching it into the fire.

"You make a pretty crappy spy," said Birdie haughtily. Then her face gave way to a grin, and a few chuckles eased the air in the room. Missy shrugged, smiling, before turning to Fin to finish the pilot's thought.

• • •

"The higher command, the thing that makes us *res upp* even more than fixing things done wrong—it's friends, isn't it, Fin? We see smoke, and we go."

The pilot nodded, and Griffons of all stations shuffled forward to cluster around one of their own.

OCTOBER 4, 2012

EXPLOSION DESTROYS OIL WELL AT STAND OFF, ALBERTA
Band chief questions well safety for community with 400 drill sites

Residents of Stand Off, Alberta, have not yet received an evacuation order after the second oil spill in as many years. The "rainbow pipeline" from the Cold Lake oil sands to the U.S. border has ruptured once again, spilling an estimated 50,000 barrels in the vicinity of the community of Stand Off, Alberta, a municipality of the traditional territory of the Blackfoot nation. The Department of Environment and Cold Lake oil developers have classified the spill as minor, and have advised the people in Stand Off to remain inside until the incident has been cleared.

Chapter Nineteen

EAST TO WEST

The girl's face was illuminated with a flash of red and a voice answered through static, gruff and distant.

"Hey, it's Bullseye! We are awake!"

"It's Missy." His apprentice spoke again, unable to decipher the response but managing anyway, as she always did. Anxious to be useful, as she always was, the young pirate girl had patched his crew through to hers, speaking into the salvaged radio to confirm her voice and hand off.

"It's Eric, Missy, you got somebody there with ears?"

On feeling the vibration, Missy handed the radio to the Captain, satisfied that she'd raised the Dreads. He pushed the button.

"This is Rasmus Krook."

"They're three hours later than us," Missy leaned in to him. "It's the middle of the night there."

He nodded as the radio glowed red again, then flickered off, and on again. He could sense the fumbling. The radio buzzed red.

"You go!"

"No, you!"

"Go get Vince an' tell 'im to get Gristle!" another voice hissed.

"Rasmus Krook!"

"I am here," he replied.

"Willie 'ere. Dread Huckster. Griffs still aflight! Dis makes me glad. Dey say you's taken to skies and breakfast wit' bears and dey say you've gone, ahhhh…'ow you say? *Chavirer*, crazy. But you's friends of friends, and *vous êtes valliant, oui, et* nobody likes crocheted slippers, and so *bon*, and our Missy found you, ah?"

Rasmus looked at Missy, holding her line of sight as he spoke. He pushed the button.

"Hello, Willie. She did indeed find us. She has proven an excellent recruit."

"*Bon, bon*…jus' keepin' the line warm, the tracker kid is 'ere now wit' Gristle—"

As the radio was passed in the east, anxious faces exchanged glances in the west. Rasmus raised the radio to his mouth, fingers poised to squeeze the button. Before he could, it flashed red again.

"Rasmus Krook," said a new voice, deep and definitive. The captain smiled with familiarity and Missy knew—now, it was a captain-to-captain conversation. Listening to one-half of the conversation through sight would have to be enough. "We have heard only bits and pieces but you've been missed, brother, union or not. What can we do for you?"

Rasmus sighed and pressed the button. "It's too much to ask, I'm afraid. We are grounded, Hector. Ship's bent up pretty badly."

"Grounded? Where is she? Where are you?"

"The Avenger's resting in a field close to here. It's remote, she won't be discovered. We're taking shelter in an old fort museum. We're safe for now."

"Grounded…blast it. Safe—no." Hector's voice grew dark, an alarm. "Is Missy there?"

"She is here," replied Rasmus, urgently now. "What is wrong, Gristle?"

"The union planted a GPS in her backpack. They been watchin' you, waitin' for you to land and stay in one spot. They know where you are, Krook. Where she is."

The captain's face went white, and Missy's stomach turned. She tugged at his shirtsleeve. "What are they saying?"

"Hold, Gristle." Rasmus turned to Missy.

Union put a device on you, he mouthed, and the deception hit them both in a flash. They'd been tracking her from the moment she came on board. By now they would know that Missy had not only betrayed the chief, but was also an accomplice to multiple federal offences. He watched the girl's face sink as the ship and crew of her future command evaporated. He knew it as well as she: she wouldn't even be allowed to refill the ink on a fax machine at headquarters, let alone progress through the ranks as a free pirate. He sighed, faltering, and Missy stood and stumbled away from the radio.

"Oh, dear," whispered Pip, who had overheard, and Taro reached out to her, but she shook her head, raising her hand to her mouth.

"I—I'm going to be sick." The radio flashed red again as the girl's feet thumped down the hall. Pip made to follow, but Taro's hand on her elbow said *Let her have a moment.*

"Krook? Are you there? Is she there?" Hector's concerned voice broke through static again, and Rasmus pushed the button.

"We're—I'm here," he replied. "She will recover. But as you know, our friends are in danger, and the union and police close in on us. And we cannot move…"

He trailed off and released the button. Silence filled both ends of the radio, hanging in air that felt penetrated by every threat of retribution that Chief B had ever hurled to the sky. The light went red again.

"Tell me what you need," said Hector Gristle.

Meena, Vince, Ike, and more Dreads gathered until the whole crew clustered around the eastern radio. In the west, with no reason not to, Rasmus Krook answered simply.

"New blades. A stern starboard hull. Raw aluminum. New landing-gear hydraulics. And grease—a few hundred gallons of cooking oil. All before the union picks up our signal and arrives."

There was a long pause, then more red, and Fort Walsh listened in on New Germany's emergency conference.

"Vince?" Hector called on his first mate, the line still open.

"The grease we can manage." The first mate had stepped forward. "There's a factory north of Bathurst that makes the national order of Jolly Roger's fish sticks. We'll duck in there at night, on the way. They'll have barrels there already. That's how the haddock comes in. We'll use 'em to take the grease out."

"Phezzie—the metal? The engine parts?"

The machinist spoke next. "Gonna be tough to come by 'round here. Any metal we get's not gonna be aviation-grade…"

Missy appeared again, sidling up next to Cirrus, her face smudged and puffy. "What're they saying?"

He looked at her. "They're thinkin'."

"Shearwater!" The voice of Sam had shoved his way to the front on the eastern end. "It's the biggest air force base anywhere. It's where the Hercules freighters live and plenty of spare parts, I bet. That'd be close to the *Avenger* in size, Krook, sir? She's a giant, is she not?"

Rasmus Krook clutched the radio, pressing the button to speak. "Next to a Hercules, she's no giant. She's a match."

Cirrus translated and Missy, weary and still in shock, nodded.

•••

With a couple of interesting years under their belts of having junk pirates in their midst, the people of New Germany didn't mind the occasional flurry of activity that struck the Stewart property—even the most unconventional flurries. Some neighbours even helped out from time to time. The Barrow, Cyril Coolen's dump truck, and John Borgal's flatbed were parked in a row in the yard. Eric hoisted one leg over the edge of the ship's hull, swinging around to shimmy down the chain net, an unnecessary but irresistible mode of disembarking. He ran between the trucks and across the yard and up the porch steps, then clattered through the screen door and up more steps, then up through the hatch to the attic where everything would be decided.

His head emerged, then his shoulders and arms, then his legs unfolded and he stood, panting, between the old man and the first mate.

"They're waiting with the list. Take it down." Vince waved toward the radio, and Eric stared dumbly. "You, kid, are this mission's Stock Chief. Eyes an' ears."

He gave a shove and Eric landed in a chair. Then he reached over the boy to switch on the radio once more. He spoke.

"Fort Walsh, come in. We are a green for transmission."

"Ready, Scotia. Got a pen?"

Eric gulped and pushed the button. "Go ahead, Fort Walsh."

Sheet metal, 2.25 tonnes; hydraulics piping; electrical panel, landing gear, nose of Hercules.

"Got it," he spoke into the radio after a man named Ginsberg relayed the list for the second time. The light went red.

"…an' whatever else looks good."

Eric pushed the broadcast button. "Like what, over?"

"Tools, kid! Always tools. Tools an' scaffolds an' if yeh see one o' those hats you gotta grab it. Y'know, the ones wit' the feathers an' the gold rope an' stuff, over."

"I don't think they wear those anymore. And that's not the air force. That's the navy. In England."

There was a pause on the other end. The light went red.

"Ah, well. We need all on that list and whatever else you can carry. For all the effort, may as well make it good. Fort Walsh out."

• • •

"Hodgepodge." There was a pause on the other end of the radio. Eric's father spoke again. "Uhhh. Hello? Hodgepodge, right? Is this the, uh, pirate union?"

Another pause, then a terse voice replied. "That is last month's code phrase, over."

"We don't have the new one," Dan replied. "Sorry. Over."

"You're sorry?" The receptionist seemed confused.

"This is T.H.U.G.S.S. central, right?"

"I'm going to need your identification number."

"52-03-01 on behalf of Hector Gristle."

She covered the transmitter and spoke, muffled, to some other authority. After another pause she spoke again.

"We can see from our tele-radar that you are on the south shore of Nova Scotia. We have been made aware of certain… civilian deputies based there. How may I direct your call, over?"

Dan, past the initial hurdle, fumbled. He hadn't thought beyond getting through. The light held red.

"It's a message we're supposed to deliver on behalf of the Dreads. Because they are in…Vermont. Right now. The Dreads. They're not here. And they said if we heard any news we were supposed to call you right away. And we have some news. Something about a mission? And somebody called Missy Bullseye."

On the Halifax end there was more muffled hissing and what sounded like a scramble.

Get the chief!

Throw the switch, get this on tape!

SHHHH! It's an open channel. They'll hear you.

"I'm sorry, did you say something? The receiver here's older than I am."

At headquarters, the receptionist dropped the radio, cursed, then picked it up again, panting. "No, nothing here, fine, please continue. Message transcription beginning."

"Here's what she said. She said the ship—Avenger? What's the Avenger? Never heard of it—"

Anneke winked at her husband and her husband winked back.

"Anyway, she said the ship had landed at some kind of museum in Saskatchewan, but they're about to take off again. They'll be on their way to the Territories—something about airstrip nine—is this right, darling?"

"Yes, muffin! That's a nine written right there. Enterprise, way up in the Arctic!" Anneke had never stirred a bureaucratic pot before. She liked it.

"The Arctic! My goodness." Dan matched his wife's cheery obliviousness. "The ship took off but this Missy character left her backpack at...what's this say here? At some abandoned fort in Saskatchewan. It got trampled on or some such nonsense and now it's there all by itself. She was wondering if one of the couriers from the Victoria headquarters might pick it up next time they go by. She's got a prize yo-yo in there, you know."

What did he say? What about a yo-yo?

The GPS! It's not moving because she dropped it—they're not on the ground at Fort Walsh! Only the backpack is!

Middle managers clustered around the receptionist.

The Griffs are gone again?

What did he say? What about an airstrip? They need airstrips now?

Did he say he knows where they're going to land??!

The trucks! They've got to go northwest, not west!

Why won't she just let the Winnipeg office pick them up?

Because she's on a tear, numbskull. She's the national chief an' she wants 'em herself...

More bodies clamoured at reception, straining to hear. She silenced them with a wave of her hand and pressed the button to speak.

"Backpack left behind...ship and crew to land at an... airstrip? Confirm, please, over."

"Airstrip nine!" Eric's father shouted helpfully. "They've got airstrips. Don't you know about the airstrips?"

Anneke giggled. The union did not.

"Anyways, it's Enterprise, Northwest Territories. That Avenger ship will land there, Missy told us. There's nobody left at Fort Walsh."

"…next landing Enterprise, Northwest Territories. W-When?"

"In two days," he replied, his voice broadcasting into complete havoc. "They'll be there quite a while, we're told…"

•••

The receptionist, already scurrying down the hall, scratched in her notebook and jabbed the air with her pencil at the regional manager, who leapt from his seat and scrambled down the hall to fetch the Outstanding Warrants Secretary, the Coordinator of Unresolved Delinquency, and a coffee. The union had shifted its gaze from west to north, a change in plans to catch the most derelict pirate crew in history. It would be a long night.

•••

"Well, blossom, I think we can call ourselves done for the day." Dan Stewart, satisfied, stood up from the kitchen table and switched the radio transmitter off. "I've never so much as fudged a receipt and now we've gone and lied to a governing body. A secret syndicate that oversees illegal activity, but a governing body nonetheless."

"All so that our son can deliver stolen goods from one pirate crew to another," Anneke added. "A blacklisted pirate crew."

Her husband was beaming.

"Think he'll mind the drive?"

Dan reached out a hand to lead his wife to the porch for maple tea and rhubarb jump-up. "Only if he's sharing a cab with Phezzie."

Chapter Twenty

AIR FORCE

Eric put a mason jar on each corner of the poster, flattening it on the tabletop. Along the bottom it said CANADIAN FORCES BASE SHEARWATER INTERNATIONAL AIR SHOW 2007. Scribbled notes and arrows turned it from a souvenir to an invasion plan. Joe climbed over the bench to sit beside him.

"There." The old man thrust a fingertip down. "The shop."

"Not there?" Eric gestured at a larger hangar labelled AERODROME.

"Nope. Too much security there. That's jet fighters and soldiers and cameras and barbed wire and goodness knows what else. But the scrap, stores, parts—that's the shop. Way over by the edge of those woods. It's not watched like the hangars. After all, what would any thief want with the nose of an old Hercules?"

"How do we get in, then? What's the plan?" Eric turned just then and so did Joe, both drawn by the sight of Zeke's head rising up through the hatch.

"Winterberry!" Zeke said.

"Winterberry?" Joe and Eric replied in unison.

"Winterberry." The cook grinned maliciously.

•••

"Cheese an' crackers, I'm starvin'. Where the heck's our lunch?"

"Dunno. An hour late so far but we got this shipment of wiring to count, then it's back to the twelve-wing fluid replacements, then after that the cadets are comin' in."

"How many this time?"

"Dunno. Fifty. Two hundred…"

"Cheese an' crackers, I'm starvin'."

The shop was filled with the sounds of winding, ratcheting, power drills, blowtorches, and the clank and clatter of metalwork, everything cast in the grey of the air force and of the season's relentless fog.

"What's up with lunch?" Another mechanic approached, screwdriver in hand.

"We were just talking about that. No sign—"

"Yoo-hoo!"

From underneath fuselages and atop forklifts and across concrete and behind supply counters, the B-squadron shift of CFB Shearwater mechanics turned and blinked. An enormous food cart rolled toward them from the open doors.

"Ding-dong!" said the food cart. The mechanics blinked again. The cart came to a halt and a woman appeared from behind it, or at least, something mostly, almost, nearly like a woman. A short, squat sort with a cap pulled down far over a round, pockmarked face, and a broad smile (mostly, almost) that revealed yellowed teeth sticking out in all directions, the front two missing.

"Anybody hungry?" the woman said in an oddly shrill, piercing voice. After a hesitation, two mechanics and a supply assistant stepped forward.

"What happened to the sandwich guy?" said the supply assistant.

"Tied up," said the oddly shrill woman. "Help yourselves! Humble apologies for the delay! Finders keepers!"

The crowd of air force employees, all blue and grey, formed a reluctant cluster around the food cart.

"What's this?" one picked up a plastic-wrapped bundle.

"Berry Surprise!" said the woman with a flourish. "And there underneath we have Berry Croissants and Berry Pie and Berry Smoothies, there on ice, and there's Berry Turnovers and they'll turn you over, they're so good, I tell you! Our very best! Made fresh this morning!"

The woman chortled solicitously as eager hands grabbed two, three bundles each and then scattered. She remained there until the cart was empty. *Have another!* and *Get your vitamins, I say!* and *Waste not, want not!*

With that, Screamin' Meena, navigator of the Dread Crew, backed away from the shop pulling the empty cart, picked clean except for crumbs and three empty cups left over from smoothies downed on the spot. Her eyes darted along shelves and storage lockers, taking hasty inventory. Then she backed through the door again, leaving behind her a host of Royal Canadian Air Force mechanics chewing contentedly.

Engineer Bob Fournier watched the woman curiously as she rolled back across the tarmac, his mouth full of an excellent berry scone. He was just about to bring his smoothie cup to the recycling when he saw the woman scurrying not toward the food service building, but across the grass and into the woods. She had let go of the cart, which rolled lazily, abandoned, until it lurched to a stop at the edge of the asphalt. Across the back of her coveralls, painted letters said GOOD SLOP.

That doesn't seem right, he thought.

"Ooof!" A grunt came from under a rescue helicopter. He turned just in time to see a welder clutch his middle and stagger across the bay.

That doesn't seem right either... and Engineer Bob Fournier dropped the excellent scone as a violent cramp brought him to his knees.

• • •

Eric squeezed through the bay doors under Gretchen's watch and stepped gingerly past the heap of bodies and over the boot of a passed-out welder.

"Reggie needs straps for the sheet metal," he explained, nodding his head at the heap. "Are they going be okay?"

"Sure," she growled. "Wasn't just winterberry. Zeke added stinkroot. World's worst case o' wind. Then sore belly. Then sleepin' like babies. By the time they come to, we'll have picked this place clean."

Pirates rushed this way and that through the football-field-sized warehouse sharing loads, driving forklifts, and stacking supplies onto palettes. They were desperate to roll out before the rest of the base—five airfields over, a cluster of low hangars and command centres—noted the breach.

"Over there." Gretchen gestured at a workbench. A selection of ropes, straps, tubing, and wiring hung neatly on the wall above it.

"Thanks." Eric moved quickly across the concrete, grabbed a coil, and ran to the far end of the bay, near the rear exit, where the Dreads' convoy of the Barrow and its accomplices undertook the junk haul of a lifetime. The nose of the Hercules—the biggest piece of anything Eric had ever seen—was dismantled into pieces, its edges sagging precariously over the sixteen-wheeler's flatbed. A cluster of Dreads paced its perimeter, tightening the load. The Barrow's hold, filled to its rafters with tonnes of sheet metal, was packed so tightly and so heavily that the whole ship seemed to buckle under the weight of it, though Eric knew this to be more a trick of the eye than the truth. The Barrow had already hauled twice its own weight without incident, the legends of such favourite feats already told by firelight. She merely hung low in the doing of it, as a weighted waterborne ship presses the ocean aside with greater fortitude. The Barrow would be fine, and her load, too. Sam shoved past him to check the suspension one more time, muttering *You can do it, y'fine old beast*, and Eric wondered if Sam was speaking more to himself than to his wooden charge.

"Easy there, no need for a tangle…" Joe, on a ladder that overlooked the dump truck's growing pile, directed the heap with as much care as he could manage. "Heavies first, cords and electrical on the top, folks."

A queue of mini-transports reorganized themselves, some falling back and some rolling forward, with hydraulics piping, landing wheels, spare rubber, insulation, and unidentifiable scrap. A flushed Cecil Coolen, tuna fisherman and one of many junk enthusiasts the Dreads had friended in the past months, pushed a trailer to the base of Joe's ladder where Eric stood.

"Found a half-dozen crash-seats and harnesses out back, and this load of epoxies, all full…" Cecil's voice drifted off as Johnnie Golden strode up to the ladder.

"Finally broke open the tool locker," said the veteran chopper. "Sula's comin' with the take, an' a new generator too. Still lookin' for a hydraulics pump."

The pirate looked down at the non-pirate man, who stood gaping.

"Epoxy!" He lifted a gallon and inspected it approvingly before setting it back down on the trailer. "Well-picked, uh—"

"C-Coolen. Cecil Coolen. I'm up the road a ways from the Stewarts. Me and Tom Corbett brought his flatbed. We sprayed it down first cause it had fish guts on it. I was there when you guys r-r-ripped down the old mill."

Johnny, a full two feet taller than Cecil, squinted. Cecil
gulped hard.

"Right. Well, Coolen Cecil Coolen. Don't get arrested, eh?"
The pirate gave the man a friendly shove, and turned and called
over his shoulder as he left. "Good show, fish guts!"

Cecil Coolen exhaled, and Eric smiled. It was almost done.

• • •

In all his years as an air force engineer, Bob Fournier had never
seen action. He was a civilian, one of those unheralded cogs in
the machine of National Defense. He went home each day to
his wife's roasted chicken and dutifully barked at the referee
during his first daughter's hockey games and held the video
camera during his second daughter's piano recitals and more or
less, Bob Fournier was a well-insured and well-settled man—all
except for a nagging incompleteness. He wore a uniform but
was assigned to base and not to mission, for Bob Fournier was
a fixer of things—a fixer of things who dreamed, in suburban
rinks and auditoriums, of action.

He opened his eyes. His head pounded, and his stomach
churned uncomfortably. So far, both his sight and his memory
were blurry. *The shop. I am in the shop.*

He heard familiar sounds of work but then, cutting through,
there were coarse and unfamiliar voices. He stayed still, lying on
the ground. His co-workers were heaped, motionless, around him.

"For the love almighty I'll hang all yous upside down and
sideways if you don't hustle! Back to deck, and bring that

generator to Reggie before this berry-drunk lot wake up and make trouble!"

That doesn't seem right, he thought. Then he remembered GOOD SLOP and snapped his eyes shut again as an abnormally large pair of boots came to rest just inches away.

"They's still out cold, Gretch." The boot nudged Bob's shoe, which lay draped over someone else. Bob let his foot sway lifelessly. "See? Tame as kittens. We can't get the windshield loaded without more hands. Gristle said to check the buggers are still out, then tell you we need more muscle."

Gretchen turned to the pile of bodies, a tangle of coveralls. Then she turned back to Phezzie, exasperated. "Friggin' full crew of pirates an' then some an' we can't spare a single one to watch these navy farts? There's no one else?"

"Air force farts. An' everyone's loadin'."

The coxswain sighed. "Fine. Let's make it quick."

From within the pile, engineer Bob Fournier opened one eye. The two giants, dressed in layers and rags, thumped away around the corner.

I'm no kitten.

• • •

He saw the boy—who wore a hoodie and had a shock of white-blond hair standing up on all ends—before the boy saw him.

"Cadet!" he hissed. The boy whirled around to see the man staggering toward him across the grass, panting heavily. "What are you doing out of uniform? Never mind that now. Listen.

Something's gone wrong."

"Sir, yes, sir!" The boy saluted, dropping the box he'd been carrying. It clattered to the ground and overturned, spilling a load of bolts meant for a Sea King's rotor hinges.

"You don't salute to me! I'm an engineer, not an officer. And it's the right hand, for chrissakes! They're supposed to train you guys up before you get the base tour..." His head swung around wildly, checking all directions before leaning in. "Listen. Go get security from the south gate. I'm going to try and make it to base command—"

"What is it?" The young cadet urged him. "A crash? A fire? A—"

"Pirates!" the man spurted, a pained look on his face.

"Pirates?" the boy said dumbly. "There's no such thing."

"Go! Go now!" The man stumbled backwards desperately, waving the cadet toward the gate. "You get security! I'll get the commander!"

Then he was running over grass, then tarmac, then more grass, buckled over, holding his grinding guts and cursing the unfathomable sprawl necessary for a base that could land a loaded Hercules. He turned his head to confirm that the boy was running too, and he was, sprinting at a breakneck pace, though he was taking an odd route. Bob crossed through one gate and then another, past a stealth jet and two Lancaster bombers in the airshow display, and fell upon the steps of the base command station so urgently that it may as well have been fire he ran from, his destination the rescue.

Chapter Twenty-one

CONVOY

"We're busted!" Eric yelled. The shop building erupted. Pirates everywhere stopped what they were doing to run for the convoy—for the cab of a vehicle, a hold of the Barrow's chain net, or a handle on one of many loaded flatbeds. Joe jumped down the last half of the ladder and grabbed the boy by the scruff, hoisting him up into the cab of the dump truck.

"Reggie! Ike! Get to somethin' with wheels and a radio and fall in behind the Barrow! Cecil! Over here!"

Eric looked through the side mirror and saw his neighbour standing at the forklift, stunned by the confusion. At Joe's call, Cecil Coolen spun round and was almost knocked off his feet by Ike, who shoved past him to jump on the back of a flatbed already rolling toward the rear bay doors. In what felt like slow motion, Cecil climbed into the dump truck's cab, red-faced and shaking. Eric shoved over. Joe hopped up and grabbed the wheel with one hand, turning the key in the ignition with the other. The truck rumbled to life and the two-ton next to them did the same, driven by Willie and already rolling when Meena leapt cat-like onto the back and slapped the gate with the palm of one hand.

"HUP!"

More figures ran past, weaving through and leaping over piles and yanking at doors. The convoy, at first a mess of vehicles struggling to start and back up and turn around, began to form at the rear of the shop.

"So Eric. How's your dad?" Cecil stammered.

"Fine. He's fine." Eric nodded politely. Nerves did funny things to people.

"At the market last week he was sayin' he got some bad wood this year," Cecil continued. "Hope it's dry b-by w-winter…"

Ewsula, carrying an industrial toolbox in each hand and a heavy-duty extension cord between her teeth, lumbered in front of the truck, greeting them with a slight nod of the head and a muffled "Mrrphhgh!" before climbing into the cab of the truck ahead.

The radio crackled with static as the order came through.

"Dreads—" Hector sounded more strained than usual, not being in the habit of attracting more than one pursuer at once. They were in a much-improved state with the union, but the captain had no interest in earning the contempt of the Royal Canadian Air Force in addition to the perpetually frustrated RCMP.

"Follow the Barrow. Back routes. Strap in. It's going to get bumpy."

Joe picked up the radio and waited for the line to clear before signalling his agreement. He pushed the button. "Aye, Captain. We've got Eric here. He raised the alarm—"

"One of the base guys got free," Eric finished. "He was going to the command station. He seemed pretty—um—upset, over."

• • •

"Damn—magnetic—strip! Not—now!" Bob Fournier swiped his security pass again and again, kicked the door, and then swiped twice more before the door to command central finally buzzed and jerked open. He slammed it out of spite as he passed through and the receptionist, sipping a coffee, muttered *If I were that wound up I'd get a head transplant* under her breath.

Around the corner and down the hall to the situation room, home of the base's senior officers, Bob swiped his pass again before pushing through the door to his destination.

"The shop—knocked us all out—some kind of ship— pirates—they're stealing! Come quick!"

The darkened room was filled with office chairs, telephones, and screens hooked up to satellites and cameras and weather forecasts and maps. Otherwise, it was empty, or nearly. A lone figure wearing a janitor's vest and carrying a vacuum emerged from behind a cubicle wall.

"Everyone's gone to greet the cadets. They'll be right b—"

"AAAAAGGGH!" Bob spun on his heel and slammed the door behind him.

The janitor shrugged. *Jeez. If I were wound up that tight…*

• • •

They'd spray-painted cabs, eavesdropped on police scanners for raised alarms, camouflaged suspicious loads with layers of tree flotsam and garbage, and split up to avoid detection. But still, the convoy was to deliver pieces of one of the world's largest freight planes to wanted criminals along the nation's busiest thoroughfare. They would not stop for breakfast or breath. One afternoon, on the verge of Quebec, Joe broke the uneasy silence from within the cab of a flatbed heavy with raw metal.

"Keep—staring—straight—ahead…" The old man was alarmingly measured, thought Cecil, who shuddered despite lacking context.

"What…?" Cecil started.

"Rearview mirror," Vince muttered, spotting what the old man had seen.

A single white cube van came up from behind, gaining speed on the long straightaway. As it came closer and switched lanes to overtake the truck, Joe saw two men in coveralls in the front seat. As they passed, they regarded the dump truck like they had the right to regard whatever they chose. One of them pointed. Vince raised one hand in casual greeting, doing his best to transmit "ordinary trucker" on all possible brainwaves. The union officials stared, expressionless, then whizzed past and disappeared over the crest of a hill. Then another overtook them, the same scene repeated, and another, and another, until a full nine union vans had filed past on some urgent mission, pedals to the floor.

"That's quite the posse to come all the way from Halifax," said Cecil. "Isn't it?"

Joe peered, frowning, at the fleet that disappeared over the horizon.

"Halifax is the base for the North American disciplinary fleet—" The radio interrupted him, a burst of static.

"Joe, come in, over—" It was Gretchen, who rode in a dump truck a few kilometres ahead. Joe reached for the radio, but before he had the chance to respond it flickered again and another voice jumped in from elsewhere on the road.

"Willie 'ere, we's on da road 'alfway to Nort' Bay. We been listenin' on d'union channel an' dere's somethin' goin' on, somethin' big, they're sayin', 'We got 'em, we got 'em!' They's findin' our girl, an' Krook, an' we'll all be...*se laisser manger d'la laine sur le dos*...! Johnnie, pull over—get Hector—"

Voices in the background became a clamour and Joe felt panic spread from one stretch of highway to another. He slammed on the brakes, and the flatbed swerved as he slowed. He pulled over onto the gravel of the shoulder, traffic speeding by with an airy whomp. Joe switched off the ignition. He spoke into the radio now, his attention undivided.

"DREADS!" Until now, Eric had never heard a Gristle-worthy bark come from Joe. "We confirm the union heading westbound on the Trans-Canada just south of Edmunston. Stay calm and keep driving. Chief B is counting her chickens before they hatch, that's all. She must have called the cleanup crew to Enterprise to dismantle the Avenger. But we all know that the Griffons are not in Enterprise."

Four trucks ahead, Willie crossed himself. Joe's broadcast continued.

"Continue to take southern routes that hug the border. They'll be passing us here and there until they turn north towards Edmonton and then they'll go north from there. As long as none of you salutes or waves from the passing lane, we're just another few more dirty trucks on the highway."

Eric leaned forward, resolved. This had been the second pirate invasion of his life. He had learned well enough that when Joe Sponagle said *Trust me* when it seemed like the end, it was really a beginning.

•••

Many days and thousands of kilometres later, Eric rolled the window down to the breezy scent of prairie, leaning one elbow out and looking for some sign of where they were and when they'd get there.

"Where are we? When'll we get there?" Amos said, his mouth full of doughnut. Gretchen, who was driving, shoved a map into his lap.

"Close. Soon," she said. "Check again if you want."

"It's a few clicks down this road," blurted Eric. "Up here we take a right and then the road ends at the fort."

The pirates turned to look at him quizzically.

"I checked out the map this morning." He shrugged.

The road veered right, turning into a smaller rural route with unpaved shoulders and trees draping over the road. Eric looked ahead. The first truck turned at the fork in the road, and the second followed. Gretchen nudged him as she steered right.

"You could be a navigator," she said. "Most people get their heads all turned round."

"I've been driving since I was nine," said Eric. "Just tractors and stuff but my dad always told me to watch—"

A sign appeared in the distance, the telltale blue of a federal historical site. FORT WALSH, it said. HOME OF THE GRASSLANDS WATCH. A picture of an RCMP officer on horseback had another sign tacked over it, hung on hooks: CLOSED. PARK OFFICIALS ONLY. The line of trucks continued along until the road grew smaller again. The wheels of the flatbed crunched and bumped at the end of the asphalt and then slowed and stopped, as did all the rest.

"Someone is dere, right dere, *en rouge!*" Willie pointed.

The convoy circled the parking lot. The dust was so thick Eric could barely make it out but he was sure, by the way she stood still: it was Missy.

"Stop the truck!" he cried, and Amos, startled, slammed on the brakes. Eric opened the door and jumped to the ground. There were others there now, Dread pirates and what must have been Griffon pirates, opening doors and yelling greetings and shaking hands. Eric stood where he'd landed, watching the small figure in red.

"Miss—" he shouted, clipped short. *She can't see me.* He ran toward her, and she took a few tentative steps. She wore an old uniform to her knees, an RCMP riding jacket covered in medals and brass buttons with the arms rolled up. Otherwise she was same as always—a little taller, maybe, but with the same steel-toed boots and tangled hair, looking like the weather.

"You're a long way from home," she smiled.

"So are you," he replied, his mind racing. "I brought you something."

He reached into his pocket and retrieved a small bundle wrapped in brown paper and twine. He handed it to her, and she opened it to see three oatcakes dipped in chocolate.

"Your mom?" she said, and he nodded. She took a bite immediately, sighing gratefully, and offered him one. He shook his head but she insisted, and so he took one too. They sat along the edge of the parking lot with unloading and disembarking all around. Eric found himself looking again at her boots, feet crossed at the ankles.

"You crashed."

"Yeah."

"Were you hurt?"

"Not really."

They ate like that for a while, and talked a bit, and then she stood up.

"Come on. You'll want to meet them," she said, reaching out her hand. A smear of black grease ran from her thumb, up her wrist, and under the sleeve of the uniform. He took it, a boost up, and stood frozen for what felt like longer that it was. *She's like a bird*, he thought. *All little and bony.* Eric imagined her at the front door of his school, selling tickets for the spring talent show. But she wasn't a kid who went to school, dressed for school, or learned at school. She had made her own school. She knew how to weld and throw ropes and run.

"Eric?"

"Yeah," he blurted, dropping her hand. "Let's go."

Chapter Twenty-two

SIDE-BY-SIDE

The Dread Crew encamped on the prairie for two weeks, hands and minds set to the new and wholly fascinating task of refurbishing the Avenger. Sam, the keenest inventor and machinist of the Dreads, never strayed far from the sides of Magnus, Cirrus, or Taro. Amos, Ewsula, Grundy, and Ginsberg got up to no end of informal brute competition, lugging increasingly absurd loads across the work site and volunteering for more. Magnus was grateful for Gretchen's steady hand on the grappler arm that affixed the ship's Herculean nose. Phezzie and Cirrus, faraway cousins in the assembly of engine parts, consulted one another constantly. Zeke and Pip cooked at a feverish pace, collaborating in the Barrow's galley for suppers at the long tables of long-gone Mounties. And Frankie, his knots of no immediate need, brewed fuel happily with Gwynne and Jesper, stirring and pouring fish-stick oil for the ship's lifeblood. Everyone was diagnosed as to talent, strength, and know-how and set to work accordingly—Missy found her place atop the patched fuselage, tuning blades, and Eric was assigned to help Fin with the meticulous task

of reassembling the cockpit once Magnus and Ginsberg had
muscled the new control panel into place. Rasmus sent four
moths in the direction of Stand Off. None returned. It was
a radio silence that unsettled him, but the urgent uproar of
productivity on the prairie afforded little time for pauses.

As usual, old Joe had figured out his contribution on his
own.

We've got ourselves an empty hold going back east, he thought
to himself. He scratched his chin, contemplating the massive
wheels and necks of wrecked landing gear that lay tossed aside
in the grass. The metal, bent perversely and crippled with the
impact of the crash, looked almost peaceful, catching the light
of the sunset. He turned and set off in search of the forklift
and the cradle. *Just like we say in the Maritime woods. Leave no
trace.*

•••

"Miss *flicka*, it is time." The bladesmith handed Missy a
megaphone. "Let's give these new blades a stretch."

She put the megaphone to her mouth.

"Griffs! Dreads! Eyes up!" she called. Pip, pulling a cart
of food, stopped to look, and a single muffin bumped off and
rolled. Sam and Brock emerged down the stern ramp panting,
having heard the call from deep inside the engine room. Shivers
dropped her maps, and Ginsberg and Billy Grundy lifted their
heat shields and stood up, waiting. Missy watched more crew
abandon stations, Dreads and Griffs gathering to sit on the

ground and standing back, hands shielding the sun. She checked Taro's stopwatch before lifting the megaphone to her mouth once more.

"Ten seconds to blade test."

Fin's voice broadcasted from the cockpit. "Blade test confirmed. T-minus ten, nine, eight…"

Missy handed the megaphone back to Taro. He pointed to a handle bolted to the wing.

"Lie down and hang on here, and don't let go."

"Three—two—one!" The crowd yelled in unison. With a great shuddering whirr, four sets of rotors clicked into gear and began to spin, slowly at first, then a little faster, evoking a liftoff but not quite. Missy pressed herself hard to the wing. Then the whirr decelerated. For this initial connections and switches test, a few rotations were sufficient. Missy lifted her face from the folds of her arms to see Taro already on his feet. Though she couldn't register Fin's voice through the megaphone (THE AVENGER IS RESTORED! THE AVENGER IS RESTORED!), Missy saw the cheering far below. Two weeks of never-stopping work had paid off.

"*Res upp!*"

"To the sky!"

"To wrench!"

As the rotors wound to a stop, Missy looked to the ground far below. Hector stood with Rasmus, shaking his hand as their crews whooped around them. Eric caught Missy's eye then, his white-blond hair sticking up every wild way. He was waving madly, a wrench in his hand. Missy waved back. Then she looked up at the arrays of silver glistening in the sun, reaching. *It's like they're twitchy too.*

And they were.

•••

The ash was swept from the fireplace, crumbs wiped from the table, and each RCMP uniform put back in place, mostly. The Dread Crew had departed two days before, bound for the Trans-Canada heading east, loaded this time with mangled junk metal. *A fine payout for fine work*, Rasmus had thought as the convoy pulled out of the parking lot. Raised fists, raised voices. Now, after those two days spent repacking and readying for flight, Griffon pirates sprinted cheerfully between their ship and shelter in the final prep before takeoff. Their captain walked briskly across the parking lot to the old barracks in search of his logbook, Shivers' maps, and a coil of repair webbing.

Then something fluttered in his peripheral vision and he stopped. The moth, beaten and singed, limped to the dirt in front of him, as exhausted as a micro-machine can be.

"*Våra vänner*, finally…" he murmured to himself, retrieving it and untwisting the tube—which read, simply, CAPTAIN—and he pulled the message out.

SIPIAPO · OCTOBER 27. Sorry about your crash.
Glad nobody got hurt. A lot of problems here
since the well blew up. They had it
stabilized and told us it was safe to stay,
but then it spilled. 2 million barrels this
time. There's dead animals and we all
feel sick. No government yet. Everything
         stinks.
             — Lou Brave Crow

FLYGPOST

• • •

"Birdie. Birdie!" Cirrus tugged at his sister's sleeve. The shower
of sparks ceased. She lowered the torch and raised her face
shield, turning to him in the shadow of the *Avenger*'s hull.

"This seam's sloppy," she said, irritated. "I can't let it g—"

"Captain got a moth. It grazed my arm when it went past.
Barely made it through."

She dropped her tools and followed him. They broke into a
run when they hit the clearing and found the captain standing
soberly, one hand over his mouth and the other clutching a tiny
piece of paper. The young pirates sidled up next to him, urgency
shrinking the usual respectful distance.

"Captain," Birdie whispered.

"You know the only moths that come back are Blood Tribe moths," he said before turning to his metalsmith and her machinist brother. Birdie nodded slowly.

"What do they say about the smoke?" Cirrus asked.

"They—" Another fluttering in the dusk and a whoosh past Cirrus's head, and a second moth landed with a flop across the yard.

Birdie ran to fetch it and came back with the tube in her hand. Rasmus cracked and unfurled it.

SIPIAPO. OCTOBER 28. Grassfires have spread. The oil is burning and the road is blocked. No evacuation orders or help. They think it's minor like other times, but it's not. The wind is up and the fire has fuel. Are you in the sky yet?
— Lou

FLYGPOST

"Wait. What? Two at the same time?" Birdie cried.

Rasmus, stock-still, examined both.

"The first one had a rough trip. The second was sent last

night." He pocketed the messages. "Fin will be edgy without more trials, but she's been edgy before. Now, we fly."

• • •

Rolf pulled the gate shut behind him with a clunk. He patted it twice before his final trek from the parking lot to the field-turned-tarmac. *Thank you, good shelter*, he whispered. Missy ran toward him.

"Rolf! Is that all?"

"It is."

Without another word Missy turned in the grass and headed once more for the path, breaking through the trees to the Avenger. The captain waited at the hold, watching, and she raised a thumb in the air as she ran. *Good to go.* She and Rolf, along with the last few, scrambled up the ramp as the turbine growled to life, a rotor-wind accelerating at their backs. The captain ordered stations, and stations replied with voices and radios.

"Seal the bay doors."

"Bay doors sealed. Ready for liftoff."

"Cam—wind direction report, please."

"Steady and holding, a relative breeze from the northwest. Twenty knots gusting to thirty, picking up near Stand Off. Advising caution. Could be a bumpy touchdown."

"Magnus. Hydraulics report."

"Untested, Captain."

The ship rose into the air tentatively. In the cockpit, Fin muttered a plea. Takeoff reports continued.

"Cleary, you have coordinates?" The radio flashed in response.

"On my way to the pit now, Captain. Flight plan indicates landing for the Bloods in forty-two minutes, once we reach altitude. Visibility will be poor due to smoke. Instrument rules for flight and landing."

Brutes darted neatly through the ship, completing the rounds of battening-down usually done before a less urgent liftoff.

"Jesper. All accounted for?"

"Yes, Captain."

Rasmus Krook, satisfied, turned to see Missy standing at his side.

"And you, *flicka*," he said, facing her as industrious bodies moved around them, bracing this way and that as the ship's wheels left the ground and the Avenger banked and gained altitude. Missy widened her stance. "You have found your legs again, yes?"

She nodded.

"I have a job for you," he said, and her face grew solemn and concentrated. "We go now to stage an evacuation. This is something we have not done before, but it is for friends who know us well. We must land inside a ring of fire, extract all souls, and depart as quickly as possible, leaving nothing behind but things that burn."

Missy nodded again, and the captain admired the girl's unblinking keenness. It wasn't the first time. He continued.

"Your job, *flicka*, is to watch for all the young people. It will be crowded and they will be frightened. Make them take to you. Show them we will keep them safe. Get their attention and keep it. Agreed?"

Missy remembered the arbour: its song, beat, juicy aromas, colours, liveliness, and people who danced on dirt and prairie grass.

"Altitude four thousand feet, enroute for Stand Off. Smoke on the horizon. Landing in thirty-eight minutes." Fin's voice broadcasted through the intercom.

The captain, his eyes still on the girl, called out. "Birdie Worthy. Cirrus Worthy."

The two peeled themselves away from the porthole.

"We are within radio range. Call Chief Brave Crow and tell him to gather his people on the field behind the school. Tell him to make sure they leave everything but each other. Tell him we land in thirty-eight minutes."

Birdie and Cirrus, dodging and leaping over crates and abandoned tools, ran like cats for the radio room.

Chapter Twenty-three

BLOOD TRIBE RESCUE

Lou paced back and forth through friends and neighbours with his hands pressed to shoulders, leaning in to chat with elders and pass out blankets and granola bars.

"They'll be here soon, Pete. And don't worry, Essie. There'll be room for your dog. Good girl."

He gave the mutt a scratch on the head and it snarled, nipping his hand.

"Sorry, Lou," said Essie. "He's a bit titchy with all the smoke."

"Smart dog." He looked again at the expanse of rolling prairie in the distance. Emboldened by spilt oil, the fire was growing closer and hungrier.

"Hey. Lou." Another voice called out. "Where's the suits?"

"Tryin' to save their other sites," said Lou. "They been here on and off since the first broken well. Doing what, I don't know."

"No sign of the feds? No provincial folks?" A cluster of voices grew around him. He tried to remember the day he'd become the town organizer. The day his father became chief, he guessed, his whole family the touchpoint.

"They keep sayin' they're comin'. The attack team's out heli-bombin' but the fire's too jacked up with chemicals—"

A panicked, angry murmur rose among the crowd. Lou waved his hands.

"Look. For now, we've just got to get to the Siksika. It'll be just like for hockey, Kenny. We'll be billeting."

He gave the junior-high school kid at his side a tussle.

"Here they come!" Essie pointed at the sky. A shout burst out from every set of Kainai lungs—activists, loggers, oblivious children, even the odd litterbug among them. Lou muttered a frantic roll call in his head, scanning faces. *No matter how you care or how you don't, if you make money or protest, nothing makes politics matter less than a stink like this.*

The Avenger nosed down fast, distant and small at first against the great black smoke but growing in scope as it approached the school field.

"Let's be calm—" Lou worried about orderliness. Some among the crowd cheered "*SIPI-APO!*" and others clenched, uncertain. Many children cried. He looked around him and saw his family, several hundred of them, for that's what they were. He thought of their arbour and the pirate beacon in its shadow. He wondered if they were burning yet. He lifted hands to his mouth.

"Make space!"

The crowd peeled back to the edges of the field. Parents clutched their children as the wind began to whip the ground, hair and belongings tugged this way and that by the force of the ship. It was close enough now for Lou to make out fresh welding seams, patch repairs, and the figure of Fin behind the windshield.

As the Avenger's wheels touched grass, people shielded their faces against pelting dust and dirt, others covering their ears against the thrum of the rotors. The ship settled on its haunches and with a whine the engine took its rest, blades began to slow, and the air set itself to calm again. The stern ramp lowered and the crowd rippled with whispers, waiting.

• • •

"Oh my gosh, the smoke…" Missy muttered, harnessed in at the mouth of the open hold as the Avenger flew low over the prairie toward the town. They approached from the south to avoid flying over the oilmen and firefighters working on the north side, putting them downwind from the disaster, obscured by a fast-moving cloud of ash. It was the perfect cover.

The ship landed in the empty space made by a boundary of people. As the rotors calmed enough for everyone to get their bearings, both pirates and passengers, Missy peered out from the shadows. Many of these kids had never seen the ship like this—not this close—let alone flown themselves. They were to walk away from bunk beds and four-wheelers, leaving all their comforts to an unknown fate, and smoke was all around.

• • •

You and your mother and me used to watch Chaplin movies, her father had said to her once. *Even when you were a baby. Charlie*

knows how to make you laugh when you'd otherwise be crying.
Clever Charlie.

Missy tightened her throat for the most ridiculous voice she could muster, and yelled through the megaphone from the darkness of the hold.

"BLOODS OF THE BLACKFOOT CONFEDERACY! I ORDER YOU TO COME WITH ME!"

Wearing Birdie's steel-toed boots with Gold Rush's uniform jacket (she couldn't resist keeping it, having left the diorama mannequin in an I SURVIVED MARIO'S DOUGHNUT BURGER t-shirt), she marched down the ramp with her chin thrust up and her arms swinging. She then tripped spectacularly, landing with her rear end in the air and the jacket up over her head. She leapt up in a single bound, making a great fuss of brushing off the dust and straightening herself. Two children, who'd pushed through to the front, snickered nervously. She raised the megaphone to her mouth.

"YOU TWO!" Missy shouted, pointing. "NO GIGGLING ALLOWED."

They giggled. Missy cleared her throat.

"CHILDREN WITH BLACK FEET."

"We don't have black feet!" Another four or five had pushed their way forward.

"WHAT DO YOU MEAN, YOU DON'T HAVE BLACK FEET?"

"We don't!"

"I WAS TOLD YOU HAVE BLACK FEET."

More children shoved their way forward and one of them raised her hand and called out.

"We are the *Niitsítapi*, the original people, and my brother Andy keeps goal for the Red Deer Rebels, so there!"

Missy pressed her lips to the mouthpiece.

"NOBODY COME WITH ME! WHATEVER YOU DO, CHILDREN WITH NO BLACK FEET, DO NOT FOLLOW ME OR YOU WILL BE IN BIG, BIG TROUBLE."

She turned on her heel and marched back up the ramp, a stream of toilet paper trailing from the belt of her pants. The children paused before Iyla Two-Feathers, sister of Andy the goalie, jumped up on the ramp and scrambled after Missy, wrapping a fist around the trailing stream of paper and yanking. She waggled it overhead, making sure all her friends could see. Some giggled. Others gaped. Then she followed, disappearing after Missy into the hold. The crowd waited, unsure.

"WHAT ARE YOU DOING IN HERE!" Missy's bellow rang out in mock alarm from inside the ship. The gaping ones jumped, and the gigglers giggled again. "I AM THE AUTHORITY HERE!"

Mary Little Calf and Andrew Lake tiptoed up the ramp into the ship, curiosity winning, their parents smiling now. More followed. *Sipiapo* himself had appeared among the crowd, his hand on shoulders, and then Rolf was there too, and Magnus and Cam, pressing hand to hand.

"Kids down below…"

"Elders in bunks and benches, the rest of us can squish…"

A plume of smoke rose from the woods beyond the high school as the Avenger lifted from the ground. Across the emptied town, black billowing columns rose high into the sky. A dog barked inside the fuselage. There was no cheering now. Despite the spectacle of friendship and relief, too much was already lost.

•••

FEDERAL INVESTIGATORS ENROUTE. TOXIC PROTOCOL. RESIDENTS ADVISED TO STAY INDOORS. ASSESSMENT FORTHCOMING.

The fax was signed by the minister for the environment, the environment aide for natural resources, and the natural resources liaison for aboriginal affairs. It spilled off the machine and curled up to roll lazily off the desk and onto the floor, where it began to smoulder. The floor of the council office at Stand Off was melting.

•••

Far away, in the distant east of the Maritimes, Professor Neil MacDonald heard the door to the lecture hall open and called over his shoulder, engrossed in marking. "Today's class is over. I've got the handouts if you want."

The visitor did not reply. The professor removed his glasses and looked up.

"Look, if you need calculation help, three-thirty is the next—"

Ike, greasy as ever and chewing on a hunk of bark jerky, shuffled uncomfortably with a sidelong glance at the stacks of books, the whiteboard of equations, and the neat rows of desks. He took three steps toward the professor, his boots leaving smears of mud on the floor, and he stopped. Then up one step and he looked back, imploring for the professor to follow. Then back one step. Then forward one step. *Follow.*

"No one's afraid of a dancing pirate."

The tongueless brute stared at Professor Neil MacDonald, PhD, and Professor Neil MacDonald stared back. Then Ike broke into a grin, and the grin became a snort, and then a laugh.

"Arrrghaa ha!"

"You want me to come with you," the professor declared from his desk, gathering up his things.

"Uhhhp." Ike tugged at the door handle.

"All right. But only because I know you'll never leave me alone if I don't."

"Ughh-huh!"

As he approached the main entrance to the science hall, ready to leave, Neil MacDonald wondered about the mildness of his surprise at being summoned, again, by pirates. The brute held the door open, gesturing to an old red truck driven up onto the sidewalk. The professor walked through and into the sunshine, climbing up into the front seat. *Needed by pirates. You can't teach that.*

The next hour down the coast and then inland was an exercise in charades.

"I thought you guys had left."

Ike nodded.

"So you came back. New England? How many days ago?"

He shook his head.

"Not New England? But you were gone, right?"

Ike winked.

"Ahh, secrets. I see. Was it a good take?"

The pirate took his hands off the wheel and mimed with both arms.

"And now you need me for something."

Another nod.

It went on like this, a conversation of yes and no until the professor had as much detail as possible without words. They needed his help to get somewhere, or to get something, or both. It wasn't for them. It was for someone else. Pulling into the Stewarts' driveway he saw the ship again, looking well and worn. The truck shuddered as Ike turned the key, and this time, Neil MacDonald opened the door and stepped out voluntarily, if not a little stunned at the sight of a set of crushed airplane landing gear that lay in the yard. A few heads turned, weather-beaten and curious.

"Joe!" The massive, braided woman he'd met last time approached, her arms full of kindling. "The scientist is here…"

• • •

Clearcuts. Overflowing dumps. Trees left to be blown down, whole classrooms of kids with asthma, dwindling salmon stocks, acid rain, melting glaciers. It didn't matter that Neil MacDonald was a professor of biochemical engineering. He was a scientist, and scientists, regardless of discipline, debate finer points of theory and speculation but agree on certain truths universally. When you add potassium to glycerol, the beaker burns. Levers, wheels, and pulleys are the mothers and fathers of every machine ever built. And we're mucking it up terribly, this planet. Heating it up and smoking it up and clogging it up and gobbling it up at a rate that can't keep on. And so when a pack of pirates, a couple of goat farmers, and an old man gave Professor Neil MacDonald the ten-cent-tour of the Griffons and their mission, Professor Neil MacDonald didn't blink.

"This is why you asked about biofuels. They've done it, haven't they?" He stood up from the table, rubbing his palms. "They've done it! They must have a lab on board. Some sterile place. How can they manage the input? Where do they keep the…"

"They've rigged up the old fuel tanks," Sam interrupted, gushing, still in awe of what he'd seen in the west. "The Avenger's fuselage is an old Hercules, about the biggest freighter ever made. They keep barrels of grease on hand pretty easy, 'specially cause they're not collecting junk anymore. They've got an empty hold, one of the biggest in the world."

"They've refurbished, yes, of course." The professor paced excitedly. "Plenty for a lab and raw materials. But how can they keep the combustion steady without an overheating central valve? Not to mention the vibration—they've got to have some kind of stabilizer…"

"Professor—" Joe stood up, blocking his paths of foot and thought.

"Indeed," Dr. MacDonald stammered. "Yes, indeed, carry on…"

"We brought you here because we had an idea, and we thought you might know to figure out the how of it."

The professor cracked his knuckles and motioned for Joe to continue.

"The Griffons are outside the union circle now. If they're going to keep safe, keep aflight, and have a reasonable chance at stopping the mega-pipelines, they need money. You told us about how important this might be, their biofuel. And so we wondered if maybe, once it's tested and everything, and as long as we can keep them anonymous…"

"A patent!" Dr. MacDonald exclaimed, and a murmur of validation rippled through the room.

"A patent," said Joe. "We license the formula, and with the proceeds…"

"Riches beyond…" The professor was pacing again, shaking his hands.

"No," growled Hector Gristle, and Neil MacDonald stopped, as people do when Hector Gristle growls. "No riches. 'E won't want riches. Not Krook."

The professor studied this leader of pirates curiously for a few moments. *Clearcuts. Overflowing dumps. Acid rain.*

"Wait. He wants to just keep doing what he's doing, doesn't he?" The professor went still. "Monkeywrenching, as you call it? Except he wants to do more than stealing mine cars and jackbooting trees. If I were him I'd be buying up land and putting up no-trespassing signs, issuing legal objections. Beating the oilmen at their own white-collar games. Which takes money. A lot of money."

Hector Gristle nodded.

"Maybe he'd like the odd barbeque," a voice at the back called out. It was Phezzie, who loved barbeques.

"An' some new socks," added Sam. "They's pirates. They'll be wantin' to keep on an' that's it."

"That's it." Neil MacDonald took a deep breath. "Right, then."

Chapter Twenty-four

ÖRNEN AFLIGHT

"It's hot."

"Lot of ash."

"Not a clean smoke."

"Where is everyone?"

"Dunno. Must have gotten out."

"When'd this happen, again?"

"Last week sometime."

"Grab the mobile unit. We'll test the air and put it in the report."

The man, wearing coveralls, a facemask, and an ID badge, walked to the van and returned to the cluster of officials carrying a small case. He opened it and followed the directions, watching through the haze of his mask as others like him talked on cellphones and wrote on clipboards.

"What's the reading?"

The man pressed buttons and held the meter in the air, then checked it once more.

"Carcinogens and particulate matter in the air. We saw a bunch of dead coyotes on the way in. This is a major cleanup, and until that's done it's not fit for anyone. And that's not even counting the spills in the woods."

The man with the air-testing unit began to pack up, shaking his head behind his mask. *Everybody went somewhere, and who cares how, and it's a good thing they did.*

• • •

Past midnight, safely returned to the far-eastern suite afforded to her by virtue of her authority, the chief of all pirates drifted off scowling, folded comfortably into starched sheets but knowing the memory would come again in dream-form. It flickered to life in her mind, a torturous nightly replay.

"We are in Enterprise, are we not?" She was the union boss. She would not tolerate ignorance. She jabbed her index finger at a sign that said WELCOME TO ENTERPRISE, NORTHWEST TERRITORIES. The gas station attendant looked over the convoy of white cube vans and RCMP cars, not taking his eye off the stranger, and spat through the snow on the ground at her feet.

"Let me handle this, Miss." Sergeant Frank Swinamer, special projects lead on the Trans-Northern sabotage investigation—quite put out at the anonymous tip that had diverted twenty cars, four corporals, a chief superintendent, and a paddywagon all the way from Yellowknife, and him all the way from Edmonton—shouldered to the authority position. In her sleep, the Chief B twitched angrily.

"We are in Enterprise, are we not?" boomed the sergeant.

"Enterprise," the gas station attendant replied, unimpressed. "Like she said."

"No unusual activity? No unexpected visitors, unattributable noise? No unauthorized strangers?"

"Nope," he said. "End of the northern line. Everythin' you can see is everythin' there is."

The Petro-Canada station, a convenience store, an overgrown parking lot, and a single stop sign. Beyond that, frozen tundra. Chief B knew, somehow. The sky was empty. What had led them off-course was either yet another dead end or a trick, and it wasn't the first time. The Griffons were not in the north.

The strange, tight-headed woman stared for a moment and then turned neatly, reaching for the handle of the van.

"Miss? Miss! Come back here! You are now part of an ongoing national investi—" Sergeant Swinamer boomed, a mess of cars and uniforms bumbling at his back.

She climbed into the van and through the closed window, raised one palm and shook her head in a gesture of non-cooperation. The engine turned over, and the other vans followed suit, and the attendant stepped aside, puzzled, while the police contingent sputtered, muffled by glass.

"I have reports to deliver! Expenses to justify! By the power vested in me by national jurisdiction as well as the province of Alberta—"

"We're not in Alberta, sir," said a constable.

"I don't care about Alberta!"

"You don't care about Alberta, sir?"

"Stop that van!"

"Which van?"

It was already moving, as were the others, and the T.H.U.G.S.S. convoy pulled away in a cloud of exhaust and snow.

"Where to, Chief?" The driver anticipated the order of the highway heading east, west, or south.

In her dream, her mouth would not cooperate. It was full of marbles, fluff, junk. The driver's face was his face then, Krook's, and the face grinned, and she shot up in bed with a shout.

"Back to Halifax, you imbecile!"

• • •

"We'd never have gotten out of that spot with the feds if it hadn't been for you," said Rasmus, shaking his head. "Remember? Summer of 2003. You threw them off our trail."

"Yeah, but it was you guys who pulled that stunt the year before that when the suits wanted to take the river," said Lou. "I'll never forget the look on that manager's face when he drove up to find all the blades on his diggers missing again."

"You plowed us a spot to land in that blizzard," countered Rasmus. "2009."

"Let's say we're even." Lou smiled.

Bodies bustled around them under a blue Siksika sky, unloading supplies, greeting friends, and ushering children and elders to warm pots and cold drinks throughout the unsullied town. Rasmus dug in his back pocket. He pulled out a

weathered postcard and gave it to Lou, who took it and turned
it over.

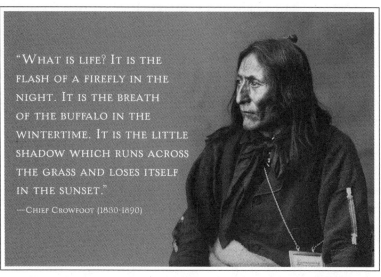

"WHAT IS LIFE? IT IS THE
FLASH OF A FIREFLY IN THE
NIGHT. IT IS THE BREATH
OF THE BUFFALO IN THE
WINTERTIME. IT IS THE LITTLE
SHADOW WHICH RUNS ACROSS
THE GRASS AND LOSES ITSELF
IN THE SUNSET."

—CHIEF CROWFOOT (1830-1890)

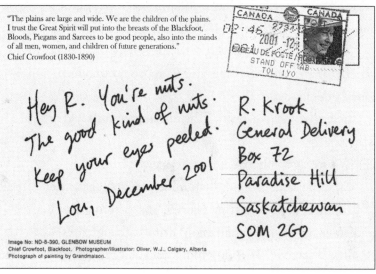

"The plains are large and wide. We are the children of the plains.
I trust the Great Spirit will put into the breasts of the Blackfoot,
Bloods, Piegans and Sarcees to be good people, also into the minds
of all men, women, and children of future generations."
Chief Crowfoot (1830-1890)

Hey R. You're nuts.
The good kind of nuts.
Keep your eyes peeled.
Lou, December 2001

R. Krook
General Delivery
Box 72
Paradise Hill
Saskatchewan
S0M 2G0

Image No: ND-8-390, GLENBOW MUSEUM
Chief Crowfoot, Blackfoot. Photographer/Illustrator: Oliver, W.J., Calgary, Alberta
Photograph of painting by Grandmaison.

"You kept this?" Lou passed it back to his friend.

Rasmus nodded. "Pretty words and just as true."

"Captain." Missy appeared in front of the two friends panting but smiling, a backpack on one arm and Lou's baby on the other. Rasmus returned the talisman to his pocket, where it always was.

"Goldfish!" chirped the girl in Missy's arms. "Goldfish!"

"You've got a hungry one there, *flicka*." The captain smiled, and Lou rose to his feet.

"Sure do," she replied. The chief's son opened his arms and stepped toward Missy, and the girl clambered from one body to the other. ("Cracker! Cracker, paw-paw!")

Missy shifted her pack on her shoulder, turning to the captain. "Grundy's about done with the supplies, and it looks like everyone's settled. I was wonderin' when we might be movin' out."

"You are asking the wrong question, *piksii*." Lou ducked into the crowd with his daughter wrapped around him, trailing squealy demands.

The captain spoke again. "The question you should ask is where."

"Where, sir? Where are we going next?"

"East," he said. "The far east. *Flicka*, we are taking you home."

The backpack slid off and slumped to the ground at her feet.

"But we're only just starting. We're not finished yet! The pipeline! There will be more spills, and you know the more they build, the greedier they'll get. There's still so much more…" Her throat tightened, thick with protest.

"You have risked enough."

"But I didn't get to see a grease take." Missy knew her voice was getting wobbly. *Pirates don't cry.* "Then you promised we'd do another wrench, Captain. There's mines and coal plants and tar ponds and the oil sands and developers and there's so much that's wrong. Nobody else is small enough to climb cranes. You need me, don't you?"

Rasmus lowered himself and motioned for her to as well, and they sat against the brick of the arena as the scene played out in front of it: the ship, the rescuers, the rescued, the hosts. A hastily cooked supper wafted out through the door of the school cafeteria.

"You'll be a Griffon wherever you are, *flicka*. There's wrong in your woods, too."

Missy thought about that. Rasmus put his arm around her shoulder, giving her a pat before rising once more, on his way to embark.

"You are at your beginning." He looked down at her fondly. "Now's not the time to be tangled up with the blacklisted. You are to be your own captain, girl. Play the union. Get your ship. Then you'll find as much treasure or trouble as you seek."

Missy watched his confident frame as he wove away through the crowd, wondering about all the times that treasure and trouble were the very same thing.

•••

Dear Chief. November 1.

I saw their ship and everyting. It's big. They came out and talked to me but then they told me to go inside to get a bucket — why would a pirate need a bucket? and the next I knew they were taking off. They just left me there. I took a bus all the way to Enterprise to try and get on board again but they never showed up. I was really mad. Maybe they just don't trust anybody anymore. Sorry it didn't work out. I'll apply to finish my third term next year. Good luck looking for the Griffons. Wish I could tell you more but it's like Jackal Joe says. All you can say is all there is.

Missy

• • •

Neighbours gathered at the end of the Stewarts' driveway, clustering to see the massive hulk that had landed in the field behind the old farmhouse and caused an even bigger ruckus than the Barrow in her smashiest, most vinegary prime. Missy, standing in the dusty space between two captains, looked from one to the other, and to the second family she'd chosen for herself: to old Joe, Anneke and David Stewart and their life of goats, peacocks, and woodpiles. And Eric, the outdoors boy.

The Barrow was dwarfed by the Avenger. She thought of Lou Brave Crow, of the arbour, of the sun dance and the drums so far away.

"Missy Bullseye," said Rasmus Krook, as soon as he had her eye. She straightened. "Our *flicka lilla*, our little bird. You are released from the service of the Griffons. You have honour, courage, and one heck of a good grip on a two-hundred-foot rope."

Vince's eyes popped open wide in disapproval. A chuckle rippled through the Griffons, and Missy smiled.

"Thank you, sir," she said, and saluted, her fist in the air.

"Watch the Best Days Forecast," called Rolf, his eyes watery. "We're going to build Labrador's first soddie!"

Ewsula, a Newfoundlander, punched a fist in the air.

"Regional expansion!" called Shivers, tapping a rolled-up map to her temple with a wink. Missy scrambled to follow one face and the next, catching just enough to get the idea. *Labrador. Practically the neighbourhood.*

"We are aflight," said Rasmus. "Off to chop chunks off the snakes before the black flows. They never stop! But neither will we. Especially if Joe and his professor are as devoted to paperwork as they seem to be." He winked. "*Res upp!*"

After final embraces and backslaps, the yard split into two camps. Departing Griffons took stations on ship and Dreads took cover, backing up as Fin, already in the cockpit, ignited the engine with a whirr. The turbine came to life and the rotors spun and Joe called through the mounting dust.

"You'll hear from us, Rasmus Krook! Let us hear from you!"

The captain, too far now to respond, waved both arms as the stern ramp closed. Missy, tears in her eyes, stood firm in the middle of the field, whipped by a growing wind, her feet set wide and her hands shielding her eyes. Then the ship lifted, trees swirling wildly around its perimeter, and the pirate girl watched as the Avenger nosed forward, putting speed and distance between them, and disappeared through the clouds.

She felt a nudge. It was Eric, a telltale paper bag in his hand.

"Let's go."

• • •

"How'd they offload the crash parts once they got back?"

Once they'd walked in silence a bit and she'd recovered, Missy was full of questions.

"They broke it down and mixed it in other junk so it wouldn't raise any eyebrows at the depot."

"Did Chief B ever call?"

"Sure did," Eric replied, taking a bite of oatcake. "Kept Joe on the line for an hour, but there's nothin' that'll stick to the wall, as he says."

"Krook said you guys were working on something big for them. Bigger than fixing the world's biggest illegal tiltrotor aircraft with stolen parts?" Missy reached into the bag and pulled one out for herself.

"It's kinda speculative. You'll hear all about it. There's a lot of paperwork."

"Paperwork? Nothin' good ever comes from paperwork," she snorted, kicking a rock.

"Look at you," Eric grinned. "You're a captain already."

"Ha. Not for a while. Got to stick to the deal, after all, since I never did find any blacklisted airship." She made a face, then smiled. "I can wait a little longer. It was worth—"

They turned the corner of the barn. Missy dropped her oatcake to the ground. The bicycle was grass-green, so bright it sparkled, and she blinked at sunshine gleaming off chrome. New handlebars, a racing seat, nubby off-road tires, and fresh grease on the chain. *AVENGER II* was painted along the spine, a skull and crossbones affixed to the neck.

"You—you—" she trailed off, taking steps towards it, then a few more steps, her hand over her mouth.

"It's a bit cobbled together, but I had help," said Eric. "Took me two months to scrub half the rust off, but then the guys at the bike shop told me to use Coke and steel wool and I finished it up in an afternoon. Makes you wonder about drinking the stuff."

Missy didn't catch a word. She gaped, running her hand along the crossbar, squeezed the brake levers, and twirled the pedals.

"Those are hydraulic brakes, reconditioned. Best for mud. And see there? Clipless pedals. Rushton had an extra pair, he told me you've got to have those, even though you'll need to practice. But they're better for going fast. The spokes are ultralight…"

She wasn't looking at him. He chattered on anyway. Finally, she turned to him with glassy eyes and he stopped mid-sentence.

"Thank you," she said, her voice cracking. "I don't know why you—"

"It was your birthday when you were away, didn't you remember?"

"My…birthday?" Missy looked again to the bike—her bike—and back to Eric. "No. But you did."

•••

BANK 20 DEGREES TO STARBOARD

CLOUD COVER DIMINISHING

The thrum changed tone. Around him a flurry of bodies, knocking, gripping, strapping down. Ritual. Another voice.

ALTIMETRE IS 29.50 INCHES MERCURY

PICKING UP BEACON ONE-TWO YANKEE TANGO.

A blizzard pelted the portside window. Rotors sliced through the sub-zero air and despite the storm outside, Rasmus knew where he was. Beacon 12. The Yukon Territory. Ice-blue lakes, mountains, safety in isolation. It was time to plan.

WINDS 14 KNOTS NORTHWEST.

"Captain," said another voice, this one at his shoulder. "We are clear to land."

He nodded to his brethren, and his nod was passed to the cockpit, and the earth, as it always did, welcomed the Griffons.

Epilogue

Blackberries'll take over, Joe had told them. *You've got to have a firm hand, but never let them feel hemmed in too much. Kind of like pirates.*

Missy watched as Eric yanked another stray pant leg from the claws of the bramble, freeing himself. He grasped the handle of the shears through work gloves and snipped through an unruly coil of overgrowth, tossing it into the ditch.

"Been too long since we cleared this out." He turned to her in the tight space of the path, invigorated by work and earth and the hopeful warmth of spring in the air. *His hair's as tangled as these thornbushes*, thought Missy. They chopped and wrestled their way through, talking as they went about the woodpile that needed stacking, the broken fence by the chicken coop, the new and completely unhinged peacock named Pablo, the soccer tournament next week, his algebra homework.

Eric pushed on her shoulder, pointing, and she looked up to see a small plane flying low. He waved both his arms and it waggled its wings once and then twice before passing overhead on its way north.

"Looks like a training run from the flight college." He shielded his eyes from the sun as he followed it across the sky. "Wonder if it flies on onion rings."

A bit of colour in the ditch caught her eye: a Timbit six-pack box, three half-smoked cigarettes, a Crunchie bar wrapper, a rusty tin of beans. She dropped her shears, hopped over the lip of the bramble, and stooped to pick up the trash piece by piece, bundling it neatly in her shirt front. Eric watched her as the humming turned to a murmur.

Res upp. Res upp.

He looked down. At his feet a crushed water bottle lay waiting for someone to notice it. He bent and picked it up. Two steps later he saw a soggy newspaper. He picked that up too. With their arms full they returned to the house for the recycle bin, to where everything, eventually, gets remade.

MYSTERY BENEFACTOR UNLOCKS KEY TO RENEWABLE, AFFORDABLE BIO-FUEL, POCKETS BILLIONS

Canada [*]

Canadian Intellectual Property Office

APPROVAL FOR INTERNATIONAL PATENT

THIS CERTIFIES THE APPLICANT(S) AS REPRESENTED BY AGENT <u>Joseph Rhodenizer</u> DO HEREBY CLAIM CONTROL OF ALL ROYALTIES, CREDIT, LICENSING, AND FUTURE DEVELOPMENT FOR A DURATION OF THE NEXT <u>50</u> YEARS FOLLOWING THE YEAR OF PATENT APPROVAL <u>2012</u>.

PATENT NO.   <u>282-19199-202B</u>
PATENT DESCRIPTION   <u>Bio-Origin Jet Fuel, Pure Concentration (Organic Matter)</u>

SIGNEE
MINISTER FOR
THE FEDERAL I.P.O.

DATE   06 12 2012

SUMMARY OF THE INVENTION

This invention relates to an integrated suite of processes to make jet fuel from oils derived from organic sources. JET FUEL PROCESSES IN AN INTEGRATED FOOD WASTE BIOREFINERY. CROSS-REFERENCE TO EMBODIMENTS. DETAILED DESCRIPTION OF THE PREFERRED EMBODIMENTS

GRIFFON CONSERVANCY ANNOUNCES LARGEST-EVER LAND CONSERVATION PROJECT

The GRIFFON CONSERVANCY, founded upon the occasion of a landmark court case won against the Trans-North Pipeline Company and its parent corporation, invests hundreds of millions of dollars each year in land protection for the purpose of conserving global biological diversity. Last month

the conservancy
announced the
largest private land
conservation sale
in North American
history, an agreement
to purchase 420,000
acres of prairie

and woodland near the Blackfoot region of Southern
Alberta for $610 million.

The conservancy's press release said: "A sustainably
managed forest landscape produces sustainably
harvested wood, welcomes recreation, and protects itself
all at the same time. Through conservation easements,
we set aside special places such as old-growth
forests, wildlife zones, or areas in danger of excessive
corporate development or environmental damage. The
neighbouring Blackfoot lands are only the beginning.
These easements create the kind of interjection that
requires industry and government to talk amongst one
another and balance the usage of the woods while we
keep an eagle eye on behalf of Mother Nature."

The Griffons

Captain .... RASMUS KROOK

First Mate & Co-Pilot ..... FINOLA PRINCE

Engineer .... MAGNUS DUTCH MOLSSON

Coxswain .... ROLF THE WOLF JAEGER

Brute .... TWO-HANDS GINSBERG

Brute .... BILLY GRUNDY

Metalsmith .... BIRDIE WORTHY

Greensmith .... PHILIPPA PIPP McINNES

Machinist .... CIRRUS WORTHY

Navigator .... SIOBHAN SHIVERS CLEARY

Windmaster .... CAM FALCONER

Bladesmith .... TARO CAT TAKESHI

Wireman .... BROCK JONES

Aerologist .... GWYNNE WICKLIFF

Junior Aerologist .... JESPER JAILBIRD GÖRANSSON

The Crummies

Captain	RIPSAW MICK MACKENZIE
First Mate	LUTHER LE CHEUF CREE
Navigator	JEAN ERIE
Coxswain	LOUIS SMELLIE
Brute	ROMEO MARCOUX
Brute	GUILLAUME GILLY CORMIER
Brute	GUDIE LA SAUVAGESS PAS DU NOM
Machinist	TOBIAS MURPHY
Slopjack	WINFIELD O'CALLAGHAN
Transport Engineer	NORAH STRAPS PRESTON
Winchmaster	CYR LANGOIS
Wheelwright	VERNIER TI-PET PICHETTE
Electrician	ESTHER ZAPS GRANDEAU
Jury-Rigger	ELI THE BISHOP BOTTOM
Chopper	SOL JOHNSON

Acknowledgements

With great thanks to my brilliant editor and collaborator Penelope Jackson, to Sydney Smith for contributing his illustrative magic, to everyone at Nimbus Publishing, and to the province of Nova Scotia's Department of Communities, Culture, and Heritage for its support of this book.

Thanks also to reviewers Ramona Bighead, Blood Tribe member, PhD candidate at the University of British Columbia and principal at Tatsikiisapo'p Middle School, Stand Off, Alberta; and Jodi Stonehouse, Mohawk/Cree activist and media producer from the Michel First Nation of Alberta, for their perspective on First Nations sensibilities and traditions. And to Sandy Huntley, former helicopter pilot, for explaining everything from silent blades to crash-landing manoeuvres; Natalie LeBlanc for correcting Quebecois and Acadian slurs; Christina McKay and Mikael Brodin for overseeing the Swedish and teaching me how to properly bark orders in it as well; and to my dad, for recommending the best route across Canada if you've got a stolen Hercules freight plane windshield on a flatbed.

Kate Inglis is an author and photographer living on the South Shore of Nova Scotia. Her first book, and first in this series, *The Dread Crew*, was nominated for Hackmatack and Red Cedar Awards.

www.kateinglis.com

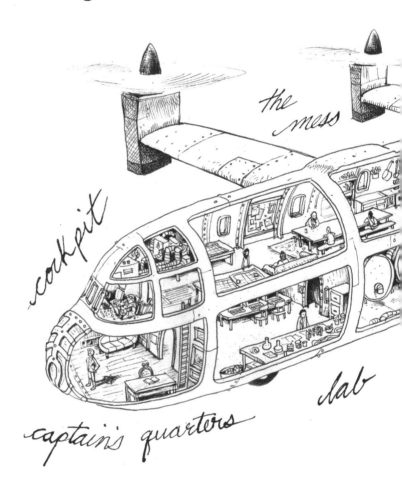

The Avenger

the mess

cockpit

lab

captain's quarters